GOLDEN GHOULS

A Greek Ghouls Mystery

ALEX A. KING

Created with Vellum

For my brand new niece Sabeeha, who might give her mother time to read this book.

CHAPTER ONE

MY NAME IS ALLIE CALLAS, I'm thirty-one years old, and if I had to compare myself to an inanimate object I'd say I'm a pocket in a skirt. Most people on the tiny Greek island of Merope don't notice me until they need me. This always involves sticking something into the pocket or pulling something out. I own and run a business called Finders Keepers. People hire me to find coveted items, information, and occasionally other people. That's the pulling out. The sticking in is when people want to spread gossip. Not necessarily to be helpful, but because they'll explode if they don't.

When they're not depositing or withdrawing information, I mostly go unnoticed, like any one of the other twenty thousand folks on Merope.

Mostly.

This was not one of those times.

"That *malakas* is staring at you," Vasili Moustakas said.

Malakas. A charming Greek word that means you've got a chronic self-love problem of the monkey-spanking kind. Like all Greek obscenities, Greeks use it equally on enemies and loved ones. No one is immune from being called a *malakas*, no matter how little they touch themselves or others.

The *malakas* in question was Konstantinos Grivas. Like the man standing next to him outside the *kafeneio*—coffee shop—he was part of my grandmother's social circle. Yiayia was dead, but stories about her voracious sexual appetite lived on. Which was too bad because I really didn't want to hear them.

I crouched down beside my bicycle to fake an untied shoelace.

"Is there something on my face?" I asked Vasili Moustakas. The elderly man been dead for several months, and his ghost didn't seem to want much except occasional conversation and never ending trips back and forth across the waterfront road with his wiener dangling out the slit in his pajamas. He'd been struck by a teenage whacko with a driver's license and a BMW, hell-bent on vengeance. She scored a new nose and a stint in jail, and Vasili Moustakas won a free trip to the Afterlife.

I see dead people. Mostly they don't know I can see them, and if possible I'd like to keep it that way. Ghosts are annoying. Something goes wonky after they ditch their mortal bodies. Their more annoying traits wind up distilled and inflicted on people like me, who can see them. Lately it was getting harder to keep my secret. You solve one murder for a ghost and they start bragging about how they know a living person who can help a ghost out.

The dead man grinned. "No, but there could be."

I rolled my eyes. "Could you go over there and eavesdrop on their conversation?"

He considered my request. "Why would I do that?"

"Because then I would owe you a favor."

"Good enough."

Vasili Moustakas and his walker set off for the other side of the street. A car rolled through him, followed by a shepherd, chasing his flock. Finally he reached the other side. For funsies, he dry-humped the man who kept looking at me. I wanted to object but this other shoelace really needed tying.

Vasili Moustakas hobbled back to me.

"They are going to have sex with your grandmother."

"Well, they're going to need a backhoe and strong stomachs."

My phone rang. Leo Samaras was on the other end. Leo is the very sexy, drop dead gorgeous local police detective. He'd like to hurry things up and officially be my boyfriend, but things were complicated. Things, in this instance, were my sister Toula and their past as high school sweethearts. Toula gets twitchy when Leo's name comes up, and because she's my sister, I don't want to whizz on her feelings. But Leo is tough to resist. The man is downright delicious. I wasn't sure how long I'd be able to hold out.

"When do your parents get back?" he asked.

My parents were traveling the world on a floating tin can. Their life now was buffets and stage shows and dining with other couples. During the day they went rock climbing on the deck and swimming in one of several pools. These were people who knew about the Titanic, watched *The Poseidon Adventure,* and flung caution into the wind anyway.

"Why?"

There was a pause. A long one.

Finally: "There's a problem at the cemetery."

"What kind of problem."

He blew out a sigh. "I know Toula is the older sister, and social rules say I should call her first, but this is …"

Things must be dire if Leo couldn't formulate a sentence. "Just come, okay?"

Vasili Moustakas and his eavesdropping were instantly forgotten as I jumped on my bicycle and peddled directly to Merope's cemetery.

The local cemetery is a serene patch of land, dotted with shade trees and covered with white pebbles, that are regularly interrupted by snaking rows of cobblestones for visitors to walk on while they're fulfilling their duties for appearances' sake. Some families go crazy and splurge on wildly decorative monuments that suggest they love their dead relatives more than the folks who buy simple headstones. The only ones who really care are the birds. More surface area for them to sit and poop on. Inside the gates sits a low, flat building that contains everything the caretaker needs to do his job, including a scrubbing brush to keep those monuments poop-free.

I found Leo and the island's coroner, Panos Grekos, crouched down next to what was either a corpse or an act of vandalism. Maybe both.

"Virgin Mary," I said. "What is that?"

At the sound of my voice, Leo looked around. Despite the problem on the ground, he found the time and inclination to smile. He unfolded his body until he towered over me by a lot. I'm 1.7 meters first thing in the morning—5'7" in my old American life—and Leo can rest his chin on my head. Back in his Toula days he had scruffy hair and devoted his closet space to heavy metal band t-shirts—all black. Now he's branched out into other colors and fabrics beyond denim. He gets regular haircuts, too. The cute boy left Merope for years and came back a man with a badge and handcuffs. This morning the late autumn wind lashing the island had forced him out of his usual leather jacket and into a padded navy blue coat that added extra bulk to his hard-muscled torso.

Last time we hung out was a week ago. We were dancing, eating a goat that had been at the center of a custody battle, and neither of us mentioned my sister once. Since then our lives had been out of sync. Although we did make out once on the stairs between the floors of our apartment building. Leo lives directly above me in apartment 302. If you ask me, he gets a kick out of being on top.

"The caretaker called," Leo told me. "Said there was a dead man in the cemetery. Pappas answered the call and mistook it for a joke. I told him Christos Fekkas never makes jokes."

True story. The cemetery's caretaker didn't have a funny bone in his body.

I knew the grave, even though it was currently partially obscured by an oversized pair of Greek underpants. At first I came here to mourn. Now I came sometimes to ask my grandmother for advice. In life she'd loved dispensing helpful tips. Bon mots such as: *Once you go black, you can still go back if your friends and neighbors die and no one is left to remember you were married,* and *If you have to touch a* mouni *after chopping hot peppers, make sure it is not your own.*

A *mouni* is a woman's lady garden, hopefully with fewer bugs.

Since Yiayia passed she'd been silent on the advice front. Not once had her ghost swung by to *tsk* at my dietary choices. In death she didn't care if I was wearing footwear 24/7. Probably she was running the Afterlife by now. Kicking butts and seducing angels.

The dead man was facedown on Yiayia's grave. He'd died wearing his oversized underpants as a hat. Something was tied around his neck. I squinted. Knee-high stocking.

Black. A metal cup of water and a pile of blue pills sat on the gravestone's flat top.

Yikes.

"Tell me it was a murder and not what I think it was," I said.

Panos Grekos didn't look up. "At this point I believe he did this to himself."

"On Yiayia's grave? Didn't he know about places like indoors and secluded woods?"

"This isn't the first time there have been problems with your grandmother's grave," Leo said. "Usually they want to have their fun and then leave, alive."

"Yiayia had a reputation," I said.

They looked at me. Yiayia had more than a reputation. Her appetite for nookie was the stuff of notoriety. A pulse was her biggest turn-on.

"We know," Panos said. "Everybody knows. Some of them have pictures."

The subject needed changing before he got around to casually mentioning that he'd seen those photos.

"Who is he?" I asked, refocusing on the deceased.

Panos rolled him over. "Yiorgos Dakis."

Yiorgos Dakis. I knew him. I knew everyone on Merope, more or less. During the off-season we're a small community. Over spring and summer the island's population swells until the beaches are riddled with sunburned bodies, lined up like freshly cooked lobsters. Merope is one of those Greek islands you see on calendars. White buildings. Brilliant blue shutters. Red roofs. Cobbled streets. Donkeys ridden by weather-beaten men wearing handlebar mustaches and fisherman's hats. Lift the covers and you'll get an eyeful of Merope's grubby underwear. Only the island's outwear is perfect. Underneath we've got crime, debauchery, and weirdoes like Yiorgos Dakis, who get kinky with graves.

In life, Kyrios—Mister—Dakis was a walnut with chicken legs and a bad comb over. In the death he was the same, but with underpants over his hairdo. Beneath the underpants, I knew he possessed one eyebrow, and that he wore one mustache to match, and the rest of his face resembled a leather sofa that had been dumped on the side of the road and left to weather for seven decades.

"He was one of Yiayia's friends," I said.

Maybe they were friends with quotation marks. Maybe they were regular friends who didn't bone. I wasn't privy to those details, and hoped I never would be. Since Yiorgos Dakis was likely a suicide, or he become a little too excited and offed himself by accident, there was a good chance he'd never come back, and I'd go through life blissfully ignorant about his relationship with Yiayia.

Ghosts have rules. One is that they don't get to haunt places until their first forty post-death days are up. The Greek Orthodox Church believes the souls of the dead roam their old stomping grounds for forty days, before flitting away permanently. The Greek Orthodox Church has it backwards. During the first forty days, the newly deceased are kept busy with fun activities like Afterlife orientation. Even being dead requires preparation, I guess. Exceptions exist. Murder, for one. Homicide victims get special dispensation to bounce right back to the land of the living.

Panos carefully unwound the black stocking and set it aside. He left the underpants on Yiorgos Dakis' head. Thankfully. "People do strange things," he said like his kinks were somehow superior. The island's coroner is one of those weirdoes who hoofs it to the *periptero*—newsstand —on a regular basis to buy his porn the old-fashioned way:

on paper. He leans toward over-inflated breasts and inserting objects in women's outboxes. Unbeknownst to Panos, his dead mother wafts along behind him as he carries his magazines home, howling about his proclivities and all the ways she screwed up parenting. My biggest problem with Panos is that for whatever reason, he doesn't get his porn for free on the internet like everyone else. Could be he's that rare bird, in it for the journalism.

"Why am I here?" I asked. "Do you need me to find something? Like maybe the other stocking? Please say you don't need me to find the other stocking."

Leo pulled me aside. His gaze flicked over me, down then up. I'd been around the block a time or two. I knew what that look meant, and I flushed accordingly. He was on the job but he wished he wasn't. That made two of us.

"Was it a murder?" he asked in a low voice.

"Panos says no, and as far as I can tell he's right."

Leo knows I see ghosts. He has issues with that, but the man gets an A for effort. It's not me that's the problem; he's not convinced ghosts exist. But if they don't exist then who am I talking to? He knows I'm sane. Therefore ghosts are real. But he isn't convinced ghosts are really real. It's a big ol' circle.

Like I said, he's trying.

"Is there anyone else here?" he asked.

"This is a cemetery. If there's one place I never see ghosts it's the cemetery."

"Why?"

"If you had the power of invisibility would you hang around a bunch of tombstones?"

"No." He grinned. "I'd watch you shower."

My cheeks heated up. "It's horrifying. I dance and sing with a shower cap on my head."

"I want to see that."

"You say that now, but wait until you hear me sing."

"When we're in the shower together you won't be singing."

I considered asking if I'd be talking into the microphone, but the words stuck in my throat.

"I have to go," I said. "I was on my way to see someone."

"Anyone I know?"

"Betty."

To his credit he didn't make a face. Betty Honeychurch and the cake shop she co-owns with her brother Jack are another issue. Only woo-woo people can see the Cake Emporium. To regular folks like Leo, the space is empty. No fancy storefront. No wildly creative displays in the window. No cakes. Sad, really. The cakes are otherworldly.

"Did you run out of cake again?"

My addiction to sweets is serious. My jeans are lucky I get from A to B on a bicycle.

"Someone keeps eating it. Probably my evil twin, Schmallie."

A grin sprawled across his face. "I believe you."

———

The Cake Emporium exists in all times and places. Wherever there are people with the slightest speck of woo-woo abilities, there's a door leading to the best cake shop in the world.

Don't ask me how. I haven't wrapped my head around the science. If it's science. Probably it's magic. Recently a dead man told me that magic is science we don't understand yet. He was a dick, but I'm inclined to believe he was right.

On Merope, in the present, the Cake Emporium occupies space in a narrow alley. The sign out front declares the shop to be, in old English lettering, *Your one-stop shop for sugary treats*. The front window is in constant flux, but it's always a feast for the eyes. Betty Honeychurch loves to redecorate, and she'd been at it again. Gone were the Halloween decorations, the sugar skulls celebrating *Día de Muertos*, the Day of the Dead. Betty had filled the window with autumn leaves, ranging from golden yellow to deepest reds, scarecrows, plump turkeys, and hay bales that were lovingly crafted bricks of spun sugar.

I leaned my bicycle against the wall.

My phone rang. Caller ID said it was Angela's home number.

Angela Zouboulaki is the island's richest woman with the poorest taste in men. She started life with nothing and collected everything along the way, courtesy of one divorce and one dead husband. A woman of a certain age, she fakes being in her thirties; a convincing performance ruined only by the fact that she's obviously circling the center of her fifth decade. I'm permanently on Angela's payroll because if there's one thing she enjoys more than money and skimming twenty years off her birth certificate, it's men. Angela isn't content to rock up to a date with an open mind and an eagerness to learn everything about her potential beaus. She wants to know about the warts and wives before she shows up for dinner.

Recently she had me peel back the layers on a potential British bigwig who called himself Sir Teddy Duckworth. He claimed to have a castle. Angela didn't have her own castle yet, so she was instantly smitten. His claim was correct, more or less. Sir Teddy Duckworth turned out to be a construction worker who builds miniature castles for funsies. Also, his first name is actually Sir; his birth certificate says so.

A week or so ago Angela mentioned plans that involved confronting Sir Teddy Duckworth. He'd lied about the size of his castle, and Angela was concerned some other wealthy woman might fall for a castle she couldn't live in. She'd asked me to dig deeper into his past. If he'd potty trained late, Angela wanted to know. Things in my life got weird after that. I'd almost died. Then I forgot Angela's request. Until now.

Guilt jabbed me with its grubby little fingers.

"Angela, I'm still digging. Don't run off to England just yet."

The buttoned-up voice of her butler Alfred entered my ear. "Mrs. Angela has not returned from England. That is why I am calling you."

He said *you* like I was poo.

With me making rhymes, poets' and rappers' jobs were secure.

"She went?"

"Indeed." Alfred paused. If I didn't suspect he was half robot, I'd say he was concerned. "Could you please come by Mrs. Angela's house later? I have a proposition for you."

I promised I'd swing by later. Angela wasn't just a client; she was almost a friend. If Alfred, a Popsicle in a penguin suit, was worried, then I was, too.

But first, I needed a sugar fix to cope with the mental image of Yiorgos Dakis sprawled out on Yiayia's grave.

Betty was behind the Cake Emporium's counter, spooning whipped cream onto a tall cup of something that smelled enticingly like a pumpkin spice latte. Betty Honey-church is a woman of indeterminable age. Her skin says she could be a teenager; her face says she's an adult; and her eyes say her first pet was a dinosaur. She's a tiny thing with a head of flaming red spiral curls and glasses that were first popular in the 1980s, but, like all fashion, were getting another shot at popularity. Her favorite outfit was a smile, and she was wearing one right now, inches above the neck of her buffalo plaid pajamas.

"Please let that be for me.

"It's all yours, love." She sprinkled shaved chocolate on the cream and slid it across the counter to me.

"I haven't had one of these in years." A couple of years ago, a business trip dragged me back to the USA, where I discovered the holy grail of coffees. The internet called it peak white girl, but I didn't care. With yummy coffee I could take on the world.

Betty beamed, all pink cheeks and sparkling eyes. "Something told me that would be just the ticket. Give you a burst of energy before your meeting with that fancy butler. That one's wound so tightly on the outside that his thoughts practically fly out of his head. And here I was, able to catch them."

Betty can read minds. With her magical mansion and her time-and-space dwelling shop, I suspect mindreading is merely the tip of her woo-woo iceberg.

Was it nature or working for Angela that wound Alfred up tighter than a frog's butt? "I don't suppose you can hear Angela?"

"She's not on Merope, I know that much. Maybe if I knew the woman well, but I don't know her from a bar of soap. If you want to flit back to the UK to check out this man she's chasing, you just let me know."

"It's fine. I'm sure she's fine."

I wasn't sure. This was Angela. Business smart and man stupid. Probably she'd swallowed Sir Teddy Duckworth's castle lies and tumbled into his regular-sized bed.

Weird that she hadn't contacted me though. Normally she'd have me interrogating a man's first grade classmates by now. Angela was addicted to men who looked dirty but lived clean. Someone she could slot in to her all-white mansion.

"Let me know if you change your mind. I can tell you're worried," Betty said. "It's all over that face of yours, love."

Pumpkin spice latte wasn't the answer to my questions, but it helped. On the way out I bought an éclair decorated like corn on the cob and a half dozen chocolate turkeys to munch on the ride home.

When I stepped out into the alley, I wasn't alone. He was there: the Man in Black. I didn't know his name. He'd never given it. So in my head he was the Man in Black.

The Man in Black was leaning against the wall in his usual tall boots and ankle-skimming coat. His dark hair curled where it touched his collar, and as always, his face seemed shrouded in shadows. How he did that, no matter the weather, was another one of my life's mysteries. He was pride. He was prejudice. Whether he was sense and sensibility wasn't yet apparent. We didn't know each other that well. He came and went like autumn's fog.

I offered him the paper bag. "Turkey?"

"No."

Shrug. "More for me."

He pushed away from the wall. "Is it safe?"

"What?"

"The jar."

The jar in question was pink and handcrafted from Himalayan salt. It lived on my coffee table now, and potentially contained a spirit. The Man in Black gave it to me, and at the time he'd practically dared me to open it. In my experience, dares usually end with broken limbs and tears. So for now the jar sat unopened. Probably opening it would seem like a spectacular idea after too much wine.

"Aren't you supposed to ask if it's secret before asking if it's safe? That's what Gandalf would do," I said.

"Incorrect. Gandalf the Grey instructed Bilbo Baggins to keep it safe and keep it secret."

"You're talking about the book, not the movie, aren't you?"

He said nothing.

"It's in my apartment. The jar, I mean."

"You did not answer my question."

"It's as safe as it can be in my apartment. Are you ever going to tell me who or what is in that thing?"

"Do not let anybody know you have it."

"Any particular reason?"

"Yes."

I waited. He didn't elaborate. I raised an eyebrow. He went on saying nothing. The man—if that's what he was—excelled at stoicism and secret-keeping.

"Go home," he said. "Something is waiting there for you."

"A good something or a bad something?"

"Everything in the cosmos is shades of grey, depending on your perspective."

"What about your coat? It looks black to me. Or do you call it something like dark charcoal or extra-dirty smoke?"

"The color of a wealthy man's soul."

My brain blipped. Was that humor? The Man in Black never did humor. Before I could pelt him with questions, he strode away, coat flaring behind him. At the end of the alley he pivoted and vanished into the cobbled streets of Merope. He'd left me with nothing except a vague, gnawing feeling that I was missing several somethings.

Good thing I still had this chocolate and éclair.

Desserts never disappoint.

CHAPTER TWO

I LIVE in a second-floor apartment that's mine in an apartment building that's not. After her murder, I discovered my elderly neighbor and best friend Olga Marouli owned the building. She left me my apartment and gave the rest to her granddaughter, Lydia. Lydia lives across the hall in her grandmother's old apartment. We're not friends but we're not not-friends either.

When I let myself in, the dead man was waiting to pounce, and he was doing his waiting nakedly, all over my furniture.

Salt could have fixed this problem.

Besides elevating mediocre food to mouthwatering heights, salt is a supernatural barrier. Nothing gets in. Nothing gets out. Not until someone breaks the line. A supernatural apple keeping the oogie boogies away.

Thanks to the oversized marmalade loaf currently sprawled across my coffee table, I couldn't salt my place. Dead Cat, as his name suggests, is dead. Formerly Olga's cat, back when he still had lives left on his punch card, he moved in with me after her death. He could be a pirate with his squinty eye and overbite, but he shunned a life at sea to hang around my apartment. Since he costs me nothing to feed and doesn't require a litter box, I welcome my fluffy ghost overlord. If I salted the place he'd no longer be able to come and go as he pleased. No way did I want to make my cat unhappy, even if he was dead.

Dead Cat was staring at the pink jar. He had issues.

"Don't even think about knocking it on the floor or I'll toss you out."

Emptiest threat ever. I knew it. My cat knew it.

So anyway, without a solid salt ring—or other geometric shape—around my home, ghosts like the one stamping invisible butt prints on my sofa could pop in whenever they pleased.

Most ghosts didn't know I could see them. Somehow the ghost of Yiorgos Dakis knew. The word was slowly starting to spread through the Afterlife. This I needed.

The ghost planted himself in front of me. "Wooo."

"Nice hat," I said. Underpants. It was underpants. Not a hat. In death, he'd pushed them up and back so he could see.

He jiggled. His misty body parts slapped silently back and forth.

My gaze snapped to the ceiling. I'm no prude, but the man was battling gravity. Imagine old-fashioned taffy pulling, but with sausages and golf balls.

"Can't you put some clothes on?"

"That is not what your grandmother used to say."

Ghosts: always specializing in Too Much Information, minimal filters, and sass. Know who isn't born with an overabundance of filters in the first place?

Greeks.

"At least put your *sovraka* back on." *Sovraka* are underpants. Yiorgos Dakis's underwear was the old fashioned

Greek variety. Think boxers, but bigger, longer, saggier. They made Mormon magic underwear look stylish.

He stood there, stuck on stupid. "How, *vre*?

"That's what Afterlife orientation is for. Go do that. Or go ask another ghost."

He vanished with a soft *pop*.

"Yay," I told Dead Cat. Dead Cat swatted at the pink jar. Nothing happened. Sometimes, when he's got an attitude problem, Dead Cat has heft. This wasn't one of those times. His attempt to knock down the jar was for show. Cats gonna cat. Even ghost cats.

Pop.

Yiorgos Dakis reappeared, underpants hiked up to his armpits, slippers on his feet.

"Not yay," I told Dead Cat.

Dakis looked around and scratched his head, as though puzzled. "What am I doing here?"

"Leaving?"

"But I just arrived."

There was dead silence—pun intended—while I debated telling him what I knew. Maybe if I gave him the facts he'd leave. And maybe sheep would rise up and overthrow us all.

"The police found you dead, facedown on my grandmother's grave. At this point, the coroner thinks you accidentally or intentionally …" I drew a line across my neck "… but since you're here so quickly, probably you were murdered and you want me to find the killer."

"For what? I already know who killed me."

"Who?"

"Me. Who else?"

"You killed yourself?"

"By accident," he said indignantly. "I was supposed to finish and be home for lunch."

Not to shame anyone's kinks, but sometimes people do some weird things to make their privates tingle. Like ol' Yiorgos Dakis here, who'd pulled a David Carradine on my grandmother's grave.

"So you're here …" my head tilted "… why?"

"That is what I asked you!"

Uncharted territory. Ghosts popped back for acts of murder and other vital and unfinished business. If this wasn't murder, Dakis fell into the unfinished business pile.

"Do you have unfinished business?"

One long-nailed pinkie ascended to his nostril. He spent a horrifying amount of time mining before the pinkie and its nail reappeared.

"What unfinished business? I am eighty-one-years-old. At my age all my business is finished. What else is there to do except die?"

"Is there anything you forgot to do? Pay the electric bill? Milk the goat? Finish the feta in the refrigerator?"

He pointed at me with his mining tool. "That is for you to find out."

"What? No."

"You—you find things, yes?"

"For people who are alive and can pay the invoice."

His mouth puckered up. "In my day we respected our elders and did whatever we were told."

"You're not my elder anymore."

"No—I am a ghost and I am in your house."

As recently as a few weeks ago, I was unprepared for the ghosts that popped into my apartment, expecting me to solve their problems. I was still unprepared.

"Leave or I'm calling an exorcist."

There was no exorcist.

He glanced around. "Where is the toilet?"

"No. No toilet. I don't have one."

"Everybody has a toilet. When I was a boy we had a hole in the ground, and we were grateful for it. Nowadays people are spoiled with their porcelain and toilet paper." He glanced around. "I bet you have a good toilet, with soft paper."

He vanished with a small *pop*. A second *pop* made me wince. The rotten *malakas* was in my bathroom.

I sprang across the living room to the bathroom. Sure enough, Yiorgos Dakis was hogging my toilet, Greek underpants pooling around his transparent ankles.

"I am staying here until you find out what is my unfinished business."

With a huff and a stomp, smothered by the winter rug I'd slapped over the marble flooring that comes standard in Greek homes, I made a beeline for the kitchen and my saltshaker. Back to the bathroom I went.

Dakis squinted. "What is that? Salt? What for do I need salt? I am dead! I cannot eat!"

When people die there's a process. Orientation. Counseling. Probably information packets because organizations love information packets. Dakis had skipped Afterlife 101, so he didn't know about salt. I did. Ho-ho-ho.

I poured a circle—a tiny circle—of crystallized sodium grains around my toilet. A circle so small he couldn't so much as kick if he wanted to. Or stand.

Or leave.

It wasn't a perfect plan, okay? I was working with the only tool I had.

He eyed the circle warily. "What is that?"

"You said it yourself: salt."

"Why did you pour good salt on the floor? What is wrong with you, eh? *Po-po* …"

"Kick your leg out."

"Eh?"

"Kick." I demonstrated.

He didn't kick. He couldn't. He flailed a bit. Panicked.

"Something wrong?" I asked him.

"I cannot move! What did you do to me?"

"The power of sodium compels you."

He belly-laughed. I was not expecting that.

"*Xa-xa-xa*! You have no idea how long I can sit on the toilet. Hours. Maybe longer. *Vre*, bring me a newspaper."

"Let me think about it … No. Leave and I'll get you a subscription to all the newspapers you want."

"Will you solve my unfinished business?"

"Not a chance.

He farted.

"Close the door on the way out," he said.

———

My heart said "gimme coffee" but my bladder said "no".

I had two lousy options. Sit on a ghost's lap, or beg, borrow, or steal another toilet. Three options if I counted my stash of plastic containers.

Beg, borrow, or steal it was.

My apartment building has three floors, two apartments to a floor. 202 is mine. 201 belongs to Lydia, Olga's granddaughter. Jiggling, I knocked on Lydia's door.

No answer.

Either Lydia was out, or she was holed up in her apartment with one of her toys.

Men. Her toys were men.

Leo lives in 302. Probably he wasn't home. My bladder insisted I run upstairs to knock.

302's door flew open. For a moment I got an eyeful of empty air.

It didn't last.

My gaze dropped, landing on Jimmy Kontos, Leo's cousin. Jimmy Kontos is Merope's only dwarf, and what he lacks in stature he makes up for in sarcasm, belligerence, and occasional stalking behavior. From the neck up he looks like someone shoved a stick in blond cotton candy, and from the neck down he's an oversized Cabbage Patch Kid. My theory is that he's overcompensating for his lack of height with facial hair. Kontos is Jimmy's stage name. It's Greek for *short*. Jimmy is in the movies, if you consider porn an acting career. The star of the *Tiny Men, Big Tools* series has no dating skills outside of the movie set. For weeks he'd been trying to get Lydia's attention. So far he'd managed to whine like a puppy in her presence and fall out windows.

"Bigfoot convention is down the street," he said. "They're waiting for their keynote speaker."

"Toss any children in the juicer recently, Oompa-Loompa? Can I come in? I need to use Leo's bathroom."

For a guy the size of a LEGO piece, he did a good job blocking the way. "What's wrong with your litter box?"

"I buried you in it, but somehow you got out."

Desperate times—and these were desperate, just ask my bladder—called for desperate measures. My hand snapped out, clamped his ear. I used the lobe to steer him out of my path. He kicked at my shins with his UGG-covered feet.

The pain didn't register. My body was fighting other battles. I dropped him and ran.

Three minutes later I was bouncing down the stairs with a spring in my step. No need to change pants today, no siree.

My phone jangled.

"I heard you used my bathroom," Leo said. His amusement rippled across the connection.

"Good news travels fast."

"Jimmy called to complain about his ear."

"It'll grow back."

"Plumbing problem?"

"There's a ghost on my toilet and he can't leave."

There was a long silence. The kind of silence that leaves you wondering if the other person randomly dropped dead mid-conversation.

"Anyone I knew?" he said, eventually.

"Yiorgos Dakis."

"Are you saying it was murder?"

"No, he said it was self-inflicted and accidental. He's back because he has unfinished business."

"What kind of unfinished business?"

"That's what he wants me to find out. He wouldn't leave the bathroom until I agreed to work for him. For free, of course. So I trapped him in a salt circle."

"Your life is strange," Leo said.

"I did warn you."

"You can't get rid of me that easily."

He couldn't see me but I smiled anyway. Leo had that effect on me.

"Listen," he said. "Your grandmother's grave has seen a lot of visitors recently, according to the caretaker. More than usual. It might be nothing but it might be something."

"Grandma's grave? Why?"

"I was hoping you had some idea."

"Grandma's milkshake brought half the island's old men to her yard, if you get what I'm saying, but that was when she was alive. Her milk hasn't been shook in years. Maybe Toula knows something."

He groaned. "Maybe you could ask."

"Aren't interrogations part of your job?"

"You almost died on my watch. Right now she'd strangle me if she could."

Good point. Toula was one of nature's mama bears. Mess with her family and no one would ever find your body.

Because I really liked Leo and wanted to see him naked sometime soon, I called Toula.

"I'm down the street," she said, as though everywhere on Merope wasn't basically down the street. "I'll come over."

Toula rocked up ten minutes later with my nephew and niece in tow. Even though I haven't met all seven and half billion people on Earth, Milos—eight—and Patra—six— are my two favorite people in the world. Recently I discovered that my niece and nephew could see dead people. Toula is dealing with the news using her significant powers of denial.

My sister shooed her kids into the living room. I was about to follow them when she hauled me back.

"They're saying Yiorgos Dakis was found dead on Yiayia's grave."

"True story," I said. "I was there. I saw him."

Toula is me with a couple of extra years on the odometer, bigger bras, and addiction to domesticity and being right. She relishes her role as the older sister and thinks she's the boss of me.

"You were?"

"The police needed to contact a family member. I'm a family member."

"You mean Leo—Leo contacted you."

Toula metaphorically circled the tree. Leo was the tree. I waited to see if she'd mark her territory, even though a husband and two kids suggested that she had willingly relocated to a new territory years ago. Toula didn't want her old tree, but she didn't want anyone else climbing the tree either.

"He did."

"He could have called me."

"You were mad at him. He called me so you wouldn't yell at him for almost getting me killed. Plus I live downstairs. I'm an easy mark."

She looked at me for way too long.

"Leo also said Yiayia's grave has been getting a lot of visitors lately." I tried steering the conversation into less dangerous waters—waters that didn't belong to anyone. "More than usual. Any idea what that would be about?"

"Jilted lovers, maybe? Angry husbands and wives? Our grandmother wasn't exactly discreet or discerning."

"That's a nice way of saying if it moved she'd nail it."

Toula made a face; her I-smell-poop face. "Do you have to say it like that?"

"It's what Yiayia would have said."

Over on the coffee table, Dead Cat had abandoned the pink jar to play with my niece and nephew. Toula was too distracted to notice her children jiggling ribbons in front of a cat that wasn't there.

"Just because she had no class, doesn't mean you have to follow in her footsteps by being so crass," Toula said.

Dead Cat went still. Not recalibrating the way cats do while lining up a pounce. He tilted his head. He jumped up on the table and resumed his nap, curled around the jar. The big weirdo.

Patra zeroed in on me. She threw her arms around my waist. Her face shone with delight.

"Thea Allie, there's a ghost in your bathroom."

"I know," I said as though we were sharing a secret. "I trapped him there."

She giggled. "Mama, can we have a haunted toilet?"

"It's not exactly haunted," I explained. "He wouldn't leave, so I made kind of a dog crate for him. Which sounds counterproductive I know, but I don't have kids I can experiment on. Should I try something else to make him leave?"

"Flush him!" Patra said, way too excited about the idea.

My sister went pale. She grabbed her offspring and pulled them close. "Time to go."

She hadn't made peace with her children's quirk—a quirk that obviously ran in the family. Maybe she never would. Toula doesn't embrace things like change and progress.

"Bye, toilet ghost!" Patra called out. "See you later."

In the bathroom, Yiorgos Dakis farted again.

Both kids fell on the floor, laughing.

"I need a drink," Toula said.

CHAPTER THREE

Curious about Alfred's proposition and worried about Angela, I set off for Angela's house.

After that, the plan was to stop by the cemetery and gather more information about Yiayia's super-popular burial plot from the caretaker. When she passed, my grandmother left behind a small amount of property, money, and a gaggle of friends who frequently gave me advice in her stead. Unlike Yiayia's advice, theirs was usually sensible, lacking in imagination, and useless. My grandmother had understood the human condition better than most. I suspected her friends were the ones who'd beefed up their visits, and I wanted to know why. Especially after Yiorgos Dakis' surprise unhappy ending.

Part way along Merope's main road, a bowling ball rolled into the cobbled street. Maria Griva was as short as she was wide, with bowed legs and knee-high stockings that frequently puddled around her ankles. Like most Greek women of her—and my grandmother's—generation—her skin had been slapped so hard and so often by the sun that her complexion resembled a crumpled paper bag, toasted in the corrugated embrace of a Panini press.

I slammed my brakes on, narrowly avoiding Maria Griva. The bicycle toppled sideways, with me on it.

"I'm okay," I said. "I'm okay."

Finders Keepers' clients and potential clients have myriad ways to contact me. Email, text, phone, a form on the company website. Sometimes, like today, they accosted me in the street and said things like, "I go to buy cheese, and what happens? They will not give me cheese for what I am willing to pay."

"That's a problem," I said, hoping I wouldn't have to give her a lesson on economics, inflation, and capitalism.

"You," she said.

"Me?"

Where was this going?

"They say you find things," she went on. "They say you are good at it."

"I'm glad they say I'm good at it."

"My husband is consorting with the devil, I am sure of it." She clutched her chest with a gnarled hand—her own, thankfully. "You must find evidence of his treachery for me! Now I am going to church to pray for his soul."

First, I needed facts. Usually accusations of devil worshipping and socializing with demons weren't grounded in reality.

"Is this particular devil a woman, a vice, or a farm animal?"

Her watery eyes hardened to beads. "The devil—the real devil. I discovered a spirit board under his mattress when I was looking for pornography."

Yikes. I'm not a fan of spirit boards. Too many supernatural problems in my life already without going fishing for more.

"Spirit boards are mostly for ghosts," I said. "I think you'd have to work harder to get in touch with the devil." Maybe have some virgins handy for a sacrifice. Or an app. The Greek Orthodox Church didn't believe in a physical Hell, per se, so what I knew was limited to pop culture references.

"Ha! They say you know things, but you know nothing."

"I can investigate your husband. But chances are there's something else going on."

"Do it and I will recommend you to everyone as payment."

I cleared my throat. This was the tricky part. When most people came to me they knew about things like paying me with money, not exposure and experience. I told her what it would cost in actual currency.

She chopped at her groin with both hands. Not to be a prude, but there's some things little old ladies shouldn't do when I'm genuinely trying to help them. Probably her generation invented the gesture, but still … as a non-penis-haver, her serving suggestion was anatomically incorrect.

"Good to see you, too," I said. "I hope you find some cheap cheese, soon."

She stuck two fingers up in the air, insulted my dead relatives—all of them—and hurried away. To church, presumably.

Behind me, laughter crackled out of a dead man's throat.

"Your grandmother's *mouni* was a cave of wonders. A man went in and wondered if he would ever come out. Sometimes he would meet other men in there."

My eye twitched harder. I pushed a finger against the jerking nerve and turned around to see Vasili Moustakas hobbling across the street with his walker.

I ignored his oversharing and went straight into information gathering mode, out of self-preservation mostly. "Speaking of my grandmother, do you know anything about people gathering at her grave on a regular basis lately?"

He turned around. Crossed the road. I crouched down and faked an untied bootlace so no one would think I was talking to myself.

"Aliki Callas," he said on his return trip.

"What?"

I looked up. Rookie mistake. He waggled his wiener in my face, cackling as I recoiled.

"*Moutsa* with my *poutsa!*"

A *moutsa* is Greece's most popular insulting hand gesture. It's nothing more than an open palm, thrust in your direction. It can mean you're calling the recipient a chronic self-lover of the masturbatory kind, or that you're rubbing metaphorical *kaka* in their face.

A *poutsa* is a penis.

I slapped the air. "Tell me about my grandmother's grave, please?"

"What do I know about that, eh? Nothing. What the living do is none of my business, unless they are pretty young women."

And on that useless note, he went back to crossing the road. Cars plowed through him—donkeys, too. Nobody noticed.

My phone rang. Caller ID said it was Angela. This time it was her cell phone. When I answered, nobody was there.

"Angela?"

Not dead air, exactly. More like someone was there, holding his or her breath, listening to me going, "Angela? Angela? Are you there?" like a fool.

The call disconnected.

I called back. The line rang and rang until Voicemail answered using Angela's voice.

Good thing I was on my way to Angela's house anyway. Although could anyone really call it a house? Villa was more accurate. Mansion worked, too. Angela's property sat daintily on a cliff, overlooking the water. Everything not white was chrome or glass. The fountains out front were collections of geometric shapes considered art by people who did math for fun. The interior stuck to the same sterile theme.

I wheeled my bicycle across the concrete courtyard, concerned I was shedding traces of DNA. A fallen hair could ruin Angela's whole aesthetic.

Alfred answered the door with his usual snooty attitude. He peered down the considerable length of his nose at me. Alfred is exactly what you'd expect given his name and occupation. I suspected he was born a butler, and would eventually die opening a door.

"Are you in possession of any news about Mrs. Angela?"

"Not yet," I said, and told him about the call from her cell phone minutes ago. "Have you heard anything?"

"No." His mask slipped. Underneath the layers of ice and reserve, Alfred was worried.

"Is that unusual?"

"Yes."

"Exactly. I hear from Angela every other day. You said you had a proposition for me?"

"Indeed. I would like to hire you to find Mrs. Angela. I understand that is what you do for a living."

"I find things, and sometimes people."

"Mrs. Angela trusts you, therefore I have no choice but to place my trust in you also."

I barely twitched at all. "Thanks. I think. May I look around?"

Alfred knew me. He knew I knew the drill. That didn't stop him from openly judging my boots.

"Please remove off your footwear."

I wrenched off my boots and slid my socks into one of several pairs of white slippers Angela kept in the foyer for guests and other dirt-carrying organisms.

Alfred hovered close by, held upright by the rebar that ran from his rectum to his skull. "What do you hope to find?"

"I don't know."

"Pardon me, but that seems the opposite of promising."

"Alfred?"

"Yes, Miss Allie?"

"I'll know if or when I see it."

"Very well, Miss Allie."

As I'd told Alfred, finding things was my jam. Every success, no matter how small, was a joy. Failures were rare. Most of the time they were the result of someone with deeper pockets and faster fingers slapping the Buy it Now button. So I was confident that if Angela was in trouble, and not holed up playing hide the *loukaniko* with her castle-making construction worker with the oddball name, I'd find her.

That's the story I told myself anyway.

My first stop in Angela's museum piece of a home was the room fancy people called a *parlor* in the old days. Many Greek houses still kept one room for guests, a space where the rest of the household wasn't allowed to breathe. In Angela's guest room, visitors sat and tried not to molt while Alfred served them coffee. White walls. White floors. White furniture and accents. Inspired by cleanrooms in movies like *Resident Evil*. A room only a population-crushing pathogen could love.

Nothing appeared to be amiss.

But then it wouldn't be, would it? Angela told me she was hunting down Sir Teddy Duckworth in his natural habitat. Logic dictated he should be my starting point.

I decided to call Sir Teddy Duckworth. I had his number. And his address. And pretty much his whole life tucked away in my portion of the cloud.

Sir Teddy Duckworth answered with a confident, booming voice that triggered mental images of men with old fashioned rifles stalking Africa's coolest animals. It was a voice that wore long socks with shorts and a colonial hat. I told him who I was and asked about Angela's whereabouts.

"Never heard of her," he said.

Angela alternates between wearing blinders and rose-colored glasses, but she's not one of the world's liars. Which meant Sir Teddy Duckworth was fibbing through his British dentistry.

What was his game?

"Greek, in her fifties, attractive, richer than Midas," I went on. "Probably showed up with a chauffeur and a car that costs several years salary."

He didn't waste time thinking about it. "Nope. Doesn't ring a bell. I'm not really into foreigners, unless you want to swing one of those Orientals my way."

"Asians."

"What's that then?"

"People from Asia are Asians. Orientals are objects like rugs."

"Right, right. Well, I hope you find your friend. Cheerio."

Liar, liar, pants on fire.

Now I had two questions. Why was Sir Teddy Duckworth lying? And where the heck was Angela?

Fear trampled into my brain and began stomping all over my common sense with its big, sloppy boots. She was dead somewhere, murdered by ol' *Sir* Teddy Duckworth, her body dumped Zeus only knew where.

No—if she were dead she'd find me. There's no way her ghost wouldn't show up, insisting I solve her murder. Somehow Angela would *know*.

Ergo, she was alive.

But was she okay? There's a lot of hazy gray territory between life and death.

I was done with Angela's house. She'd left Merope to verbally flog Sir Teddy Duckworth for lying about his castle situation and hadn't returned. He was the thread I needed to pull next.

What did I know?

Two things. That Sir Teddy Duckworth was a liar, and that Angela's cell phone had dialed my number.

Butt dial or a call for help? And if it was a butt dial, was it her butt or someone else's cheeks? Accessing phone location data in another country was beyond my skillset. Which meant I had to appeal to a higher power. Luckily that higher power and I were tight.

Alfred rematerialized the way only a butler could: silently and suddenly enough to stab me with guilt. I'd done nothing wrong, but his butler-ish expression suggested that he'd caught me in the act of littering.

"Did you find what you hoped to find?"

"Yes and no."

"That is not an answer."

"Wrong. It's two answers combined into one."

His nostrils flared. "Whatever it takes to find Mrs.

Angela, you find her. I have money saved for a rainy day. A modest amount of money."

Taking his money was out of the question. Angela and I were almost friends. She was one of the reasons I could afford so much cake.

"Put your checkbook away," I told him. "Angela is more than a client to me. She's practically a friend."

"And Mrs. Angela has exceeded all my expectations as an employer."

High praise indeed from a man born to buttle.

"I *will* find her."

I crossed my heart, hoped to die, stick a needle in my eye. Alfred's expression said I needed one-on-one time in a straitjacket.

"Americans," he said.

Not entirely American. My heritage was a hundred percent Greek, but one of my passports said I belonged to the USA. For the first half of my life I ate Pop Tarts in secret when my parents weren't looking, and attended elementary school, middle school, and high school, not *dimitiko, gymnasio, lykeio*. Then one day my family uprooted our American life to flit back to Merope when Yiayia called to say she had, in her words, *mouni* cancer. Cancer turned out to be something easily curable with antibiotics and a brief period of abstinence.

After Alfred extracted several more promises out of me, and pelted me with looks slightly less disdainful than usual, I rode back to the Cake Emporium for something sweet to seal the deal.

"Back again?" Betty said, rounding the counter to hug me.

"I'm on a mission."

"If you want to sweeten someone up, you've come to the right place."

I selected several tasty treats from the cold cabinets. Betty got to work boxing. As a fancy, final touch, she dragged ribbon along a knife's edge.

"He loves you, that one does," she said. "Looks at you like the daughter he never had."

"Daughter or not, he'll disown me if I show up without food."

She paused for a moment, head tilted. Then a smile broke out all over her face. Her eyes sparkled. "I know just the thing." She darted out back to the kitchen. When she reappeared it was with pie. And not just any pie.

"Pumpkin," she said. "Just like his Grandma used to make."

"His actual grandmother or any random American grandma?"

She boxed up the pie. "His. Don't ask me how. I just do the selling around here. Jack makes the magic happen all by his lonesome."

Jack Honeychurch is Merope's own Sasquatch. An elusive, magical Bigfoot I've never so much as glimpsed on all my trips to the Cake Emporium and its kitchen. If sugar is involved, Jack Honeychurch can spin it into gold. Betty reads minds. Jack reads appetites.

Both boxes fit like a charm in my bicycle's basket. Off I pedaled to Sam Washington's house, to discuss locating the current whereabouts of Angela's cell phone.

Sam Washington is my old boss. I started out as his intern, fetching coffee and taking notes. Eventually he upgraded me to sidekick, after he realized people will tell a hungry-looking girl things they won't tell a well-fed man. Sam is tall, lean, black, and warm for Luther Vandross's form. Of course, these days Luther's form is probably ash, but Sam's love is eternal.

American born, Sam landed in Merope while investigating a missing persons case. He fell in love with the post-card pretty views and the universal healthcare, and when a cottage went on sale, he snapped it up and moved in.

Sam quit the private investigating gig soon after I opened Finders Keepers. He traded in his magnifying glass and deerstalker hat for college courses when he bounced off a car with a seven-year-old kid behind the wheel. The boy's grandmother was too blind to realize she'd picked the wrong grandchild to ferry her to the market. Now Sam rolls around Merope in a wheelchair. When he's not rolling he's hacking. The man is educated out the wazoo. Took every computer related college course he could get his mitts on after the accident, and now he's unstoppable.

Comes in handy when I hit a virtual brick wall.

I held the Cake Emporium boxes at Sam's eye level. The door opened. Sam got an eyeful of cake boxes.

"Get in here before you let the cold in," he said. "What's in the boxes? Do I smell pumpkin?"

"Just like Grandma used to make, or so I heard."

His face said he wasn't buying it. "Nobody on this Earth could make pie like my grandma, but I'll try it all the same. Never can say no to pumpkin pie."

I got to work easing two generous slices of pie onto two plates along with a pair of forks. In the absence of a knife, Sam cut the tip off his slice with the fork's edge.

Wonder spread across his face. He made a happy sound. "I'll be goddamned," he said. "This is my grand-ma's pie."

Another one of Jack Honeychurch's baking miracles.

"Huh," I said. "How 'bout that."

Sam's eyes narrowed. "What's the pie all about?"

"Can't I just bring you pie?"

"Ha! The pie is special. The pie means business. So you may as well just go ahead and tell me while I stuff this into my mouth. I don't know how you got your hands on her pie recipe, seeing as how she's been gone almost as long as you've been alive, but I won't look gift pie in the mouth."

"Angela Zouboulaki's cellphone. I need to find it."

His eyebrows jumped halfway up his forehead. He stopped scarfing down pie. "You bring my Grandma's pie and you don't even use it on a challenge? Girl, I can find her phone in my sleep."

"Any chance you could do it before then?"

He laughed. "There's not much I wouldn't do for this pie." He sat the pie on his lap and rolled toward his home office. "Come on, then."

Sam's home office is a technophile's dream. State of the art hardware, the sterile edges softened by the framed Luther Vandross posters on the walls. Huge screens. Tiny ones, too. Blue shutters rattled rhythmically on the outside of the room's window. The wind was picking up.

He rolled up to the desk. Slid his finger around a track pad. Tapped the keyboard. A globe appeared on the screen.

"What's the phone number?"

I read off the digits and waited for him to plug them in. TV had taught me that the globe would swivel and zoom in until we were looking at a grid.

Didn't happen.

The globe vanished. The screen went dark, except for an address in the United Kingdom.

Sam gestured at the screen. "There's your friend's phone. Can't say if she's there with it. Don't need to sugar coat it for you because you know nobody takes more than five steps without their phone, these days."

I knew, whether I wanted to or not. I was staring down the barrel of a missing person's case. The way to get through it without panicking was to work the case I would any other. Instead of a rare book or knick-knack, the target was Angela.

"You need the address?" Sam asked.

"No. I already have it."

Sir Teddy Duckworth's house. Angela was there—or her phone was.

"So what are you going to do with it?"

"I guess I'm going to England."

"You want more of that pie before you go?"

"No, pumpkin pie isn't my favorite. Now if it were cherry …"

"You get out of here with that potty mouth, slandering my grandma's pie that way."

"More for you," I said.

He grinned. "Go on then, get out of here. I've got some eating to do."

I skedaddled.

Mentally I was working on flight schedules. First I'd need a way off Merope, which meant waiting until morning for the ferry to Mykonos. After that, a second ferry to Athens. Then the airport.

My phone rang.

Betty bubbled words into my ear. "As luck would have it, I can get you to England as quick as walking through a door. There's even a car or two at home that doesn't see much use. Jack and I would be grateful if you'd take one of them out for a spin to keep everything running in tiptop shape."

The Honeychurch siblings commute to work daily, from England to Merope. They could not, would not, on a plane or train, but open a certain set of French doors with a garden view and you'd wind up in the Cake Emporium's kitchen.

My brain refused to wrap itself around the logic of it all, so I decided it was best to accept the weirdness.

"You're a lifesaver."

Possibly literally, although I didn't say that. Betty being Betty, she'd probably already heard me think it. "When is a good time?"

"Whenever you're ready, swing by. And stop thinking about ways to repay me. You're a friend, aren't you? Although if you ever encounter one of Zeus's thunderbolts in the wild, I wouldn't be upset. I know a collector who would pay us both handsomely for it."

CHAPTER FOUR

TRAVEL MEANT PLANNING. Even skipping through a portal required thought. One doesn't simply walk in to the UK. You have to pack snacks and an umbrella.

Which was why I was stuffing things into a backpack.

"Going somewhere?" Yiorgos Dakis wanted to know. He was still on my toilet, hopefully regretting his Afterlife choices.

"Yes."

"Where?"

"Are you my mother now?"

"Can I leave the toilet?"

"That depends," I said. "Are you going to go far, far away and never come back?"

"No."

I hooked my foot on the bedroom door and slammed it shut.

He went quiet for a moment while I located my passport and hung the pouch around my neck. Most likely I wouldn't need it, but I'm a good girl scout. Fortune favors the prepared.

"*Vre*, do you have a cat?" Yiorgos Dakis called out. The bedroom door was a volume button, not mute, damn it.

"What?"

"A cat."

"Big, beefy, looks like he fought a gang of pirates and won?"

There was a pause before he answered. "Yes."

"Maybe. Why?"

"He is using my leg as a scratching post."

I yanked open the bedroom door and stuck my head in the bathroom just in time to see Dead Cat drag his claws from Yiorgos Dakis' knee to his ankle, smirking as hard as a cat can smirk.

Tuna and treats were out of the question—they'd fall straight through him—but I could definitely rustle up a cardboard box. Cats don't lose their addiction to boxes just because they're ghosts.

"Who's a good kitty?" I cooed.

"This animal is a Turk!"

Dead Cat didn't need my help. He rocked at being obnoxious all by himself.

Mentally working through my to-do list again, I let myself out of my apartment.

The door to 201 flew open. My neighbor Lydia swished out, all blond hair and lashings of red lipstick and liquid eyeliner. Her grandmother had favored twinsets and mid-calf skirts. Lydia regularly dresses like she's on her way to whip daddy for being a bad, bad boy. Today was no different. Whoever sold her the dress ripped her off because half of it was missing. Hopefully she hadn't paid full price.

"What are you doing?" I asked her, because Greeks never ask people about their feelings. Feelings aren't gossip worthy. Actions are.

She ignored my question, focusing on my backpack. "Business or pleasure?"

"Missing person's case."

"More than once my mother called the police to file a missing persons report. Do you know where I was, every single time?"

"Missing?"

"In my room."

Lydia's adopted mother's grip on reality is flimsier than cling wrap. Part of the problem is booze and pills. The rest is just her mother.

Lydia's birth mother lives here on Merope, and she's another bucket of issues, what with being raised by a murderer and all. Considering the combined power of nature and nurture, it was a miracle Lydia was this normal.

"So you're saying my missing person is in her room?"

She shrugged. "Just making conversation."

One pivot on a vicious heel later she was on her way to who knows where. I wasn't her keeper, and she didn't volunteer.

"*Psst!*"

The noise came from the stairs. My eyes naturally rolled toward the ceiling. On the way up, my gaze snagged on Jimmy Kontos, peeking down from the next floor.

"What's up, stalker? Oh wait, not you, on account of how you're a *nanos*."

Nanos is a derogatory Greek word for a little person or dwarf. I'd never use it on anyone else, but Jimmy Kontos more than earned the word.

"Where are you going, Shrek? Back to your swamp?"

I put on a show of glancing over one shoulder, then the other. "I thought I heard a man talking, but turns out it's just you."

"My feelings would be hurt if I had any."

Because I'm mature, I flipped him off with both hands so nothing got lost in translation.

Jimmy scoffed. "Last time someone flipped me off I sat on her finger."

"And you tell people?"

"Papa needed new shoes."

"Try the children's department. They're cheaper."

On that note, I took off. I stopped halfway down the stairs when it was obvious my footsteps weren't alone. I wheeled around.

"What do you want?"

"I'm not following *you*, am I?"

I squinted. What the heck was he wearing now? "Is that a fur coat?"

"It's winter. What do you expect me to wear? I'm small, I lose a lot of body heat quickly, like a baby."

"Are you creeping around after Lydia again?"

"I'm not creeping! I just want to get to know her, so I'm following her."

"Where I come from, that's called stalking."

"You don't know anything. It's not stalking. It's advertising. If she sees me around enough, eventually she'll get hungry for some Jimmy Kontos. That's how advertising words."

As far as excuses went, that was … actually kind of smart. I shook my head anyway, sighed like he was crushing my lungs, and grabbed my bicycle.

"*Vre*," he called out after me, "did she say where she was going?"

"No, and I didn't ask because I'm not a stalker and I don't care what a grown woman does with her time."

I wheeled my bicycle down to the curb just as Leo pulled up in his cop car. He rolled down the passenger window.

"I'm on my way to the cemetery. Can you ride along?"

"Wow, sounds like a hot date. What's next? Making out at the morgue?"

I expected him to grin. He didn't.

"There's a problem."

"Another body on my grandmother's grave?"

He made a face. Not a good one. "No."

"Well, that's a positive thing, right? Nobody wants more dead people, unless they're your mortal enemies or people who cut you off in traffic."

Leo said nothing at first. Then: "Remind me never to cut you off in traffic." He went quiet again for a moment. "Come with me. It's important."

My hands shook as I wheeled my bicycle back to the lobby where it lived when I wasn't peddling around the island. Winter was coming on hard, fast, and early. I angled into Leo's car and set my backpack down between my feet.

He eyed the bag before pulling away from the curb. "Going somewhere?"

"Quick trip to the United Kingdom."

"How quick are we talking about?"

My teeth bit down on my lip as I did mental math. Leo already had difficulties with my ability to see ghosts, although the man was trying, but Betty's portal to other places might make him think I'd gone full lunatic.

"Angela may or may not be missing, and her butler wants me to look for her. I'm following a lead."

"Foul play?"

"I don't know." Angela is the stupid kind of smart. She's got business brains and cunning, but the emotional intelligence of a flip-flop. Which is why she uses Finders Keepers to vet her romances.

"I have contacts in the UK, if you run into trouble."

I gave him a grateful smile. Leo is one of the good ones, a solid man who does what needs doing. He's a Swiss Army Knife combined with a heated blanket, in sexy human form.

"So what's going on?"

"You'll see."

He pulled into the cemetery's postage stamp parking lot. Constable Pappas' motorcycle was already here. Whatever was going on it was a two-cop emergency. The young cop was jiggling in place, gloved hands in coat pockets. Winter was starting to throw its weight around, flinging frigid winds over Merope's head.

"Allie," Pappas said when he spotted me. "You're here, too." He shot Leo a furtive look.

What was that all about?

Leo tilted his head. "Show us what you've got."

Pappas took off across the cemetery in a direction I didn't like. Unless I was mistaken, which I hoped I was, we were headed for my grandmother's grave. Leo had already nixed the idea of a second body, so what was going on?

The picture didn't clear up until we were almost on my grandmother's grave. Or what had been in her grave. Messy mounds of dirt hinted at the secret.

Someone—someone with a backhoe—had bitten down on six feet of dirt and scooped out the coffin. No coffin. Ergo: no Yiayia.

Scant sheets of soil flicked me in the face. Thanks, wind.

"Huh," I said. Mostly because I couldn't think of anything more apt. They didn't make greeting card phrases for family members affected by grave robberies. Could be it was an untapped market. Hallmark needed to know about this as soon as possible. "I'm guessing this isn't a zombie situation."

"She would have clawed her way out before now," Pappas said.

"There is no such thing as zombies," Leo said, although I noticed he glanced sideways at me before flopping that statement out into the world. He was … maybe right, for all I knew. Look, I couldn't definitively say zombies weren't real when my life was weird and getting weirder by the minute.

I circled the open grave, trying not to think too hard about my family connection to the missing coffin and contents. There were tracks on the ground. Someone had rolled heavy machinery over the loose gravel. I crouched down beside the pile of dirt and wondered what the thief wanted with Yiayia. None of the possibilities were good.

"I'm sorry," Leo said.

"Why? You didn't take her, did you?"

"I'm sorry you have to deal with this. Robbing graves is one of the lowest forms of crime."

"For what it's worth, my grandmother would probably find this hilarious."

He almost smiled. "She gave me a bucket full of condoms once, did you know?"

"A whole bucket? I didn't realize you and my sister were that … active."

Of all the things I wanted to think about, Leo banging my sister wasn't one of them. So I concentrated on the empty grave and the marks in the side that suggested ropes or ladders. Whoever stole Yiayia, they had to have gotten the casket out somehow. I was pretty sure they couldn't have magicked it out. Although I was less sure of that than I used to be.

"We weren't," Leo said. "When we broke up the bucket was full."

"And now?"

"I have the bucket."

Yikes.

He turned to Constable Pappas, who was avoiding eye contact with the grave.

"What do we know?"

"This is my first body theft, I know that," Pappas said.

I looked up at Leo, who shrugged. "We don't get a lot of stolen bodies," he said. "Not after they're buried."

The blood drained out of Pappas's face. He bolted for a patch of unruly bushes under a canopy of tree shade and hunched over. He made noises like a dog horking up grass.

"Good news," I called out, "you made it to the bushes this time."

Head down, Pappas waved. His body heaved again. After a second bout he came jogging back.

"We've got a problem," he said. "There's a body in the bushes. That's why I threw up twice."

"Allie's grandmother?" Leo asked.

"Not unless her grandmother was a man."

They looked at me.

"Honestly, when it comes to my grandmother anything is possible," I said. "But I'm fairly sure she was a woman."

Leo followed Pappas back to the bushes. Since nobody told me to stay put, I tagged along. Bodies were starting to become a habit. I'd seen more these past few months than in the thirty years prior.

Coincidences make me uncomfortable. Probably because they rarely are. This one made the back of my neck prickle. A sign that things were about to get sticky.

I knew the dead man. Konstantinos Grivas. Naked. A spirit board wedged under his bare backside. Probably the same spirit board that led his wife Maria to accost me in the street earlier.

Maybe she had a reason to be worried.

"Kyrios Grivas," Leo said.

"What's that under his *kolos*?" Pappas asked.

"Spirit board," I said. "People use them to freak out their friends and occasionally commune with the dead in horror movies."

"Call Grekos," Leo told Pappas. "Tell him we've got another body."

While Pappas was busy updating the island's coroner, Leo led me away from the body.

"Do they work?" he wanted to know.

"Spirit boards?"

"Yeah."

"Maybe. Maybe not. I've never needed one to talk to ghosts. Do you think he has something to do with my … with the grave robbery?"

"That's something we'll consider."

The toe of my boot ground into the dirt from Yiayia's grave. "Look, there's something you should know."

"I'm going to hate this, aren't ?"

I rocked my hand side to side. "Maria Griva approached me earlier. She said she believed Kyrios Grivas was consorting with the devil, and she wanted me to investigate." Leo's gaze fixed on my nose. I plowed on. "I told her spirit boards are only for ghosts, but I just realized maybe I gave her bad information."

Leo kept on staring.

"What?" I said.

"You're serious, aren't you?"

"There's a dead man in the bushes and someone stole my grandmother, so yes, I'm serious."

He shook his head, blew out a sigh, and shifted his focus to a distant point beyond my shoulder. An ominously gnarled olive tree, if memory served.

"I can't believe I'm going to ask this, but can you find out more about these spirit boards?"

At this very moment my backpack was sitting in his cop car. My plans for the afternoon were to portal to the United Kingdom in search of Angela. Now someone had dug up Yiayia and dumped a dead man a couple of meters from her empty grave.

What to do?

Angela maybe needed my help, if she wasn't happily bonking Sir Teddy in the shade of his model castles. Alfred had extracted a number of promises out of me to find his missing employer. But the universe being the universe, a cosmic flying wrench had landed in the middle of my neatly, albeit hastily made plans.

As the eldest grandchild, Toula was the natural heir to these sorts of problems. Except Toula was bad at things like death and body snatching. In her world things like that just weren't done. She had compartments for most things, but most things didn't extend to unauthorized exhumations. Normally this would be our parents' bailiwick. Alas, they were currently seeing the world from the deck of a floating hotel. So I couldn't expect them to boat-hop until they reached Merope.

Which left me.

"I will take your questions to Mordor, though I do not know the way." A laugh burbled out of me. "Sorry," I said. "No one has ever stolen my grandmother's body before. At least not after she was dead. I'll ask Betty about the spirit board. She knows things."

"Do you need a ride?"

"I can walk."

He didn't look convinced, but I was determined to grab my backpack and schlep to the Cake Emporium so he could stay and deal with Grivas' body. Betty was expecting me anyway. I'd have to decline her magic portal offer, but I'd make it up to her with questions and a larger order of cakes. At this point I was working just to feed my cake habit.

"Let me know what you find out."

"You do the same."

He was on the job, but that didn't mean Leo was all business. He pulled me to him, tucked me under his chin for a long moment. Then he kissed me softly before switching back to cop mode. It was all the encouragement my knees needed to turn to mush.

Backpack over my shoulders, I took off for the Cake Emporium. Betty, bless her, was waiting with a steaming pumpkin spice latte and a stack of glazed doughnuts.

"Don't you fret about your figure, love. I know you hiked across half the island with that backpack on, so you've already made room for these."

Doughnut first. Bad news second. The former were warm and fresh, with the slightest crackle in the glaze as my teeth sank through to the soft dough.

"I can't go to England just yet," I said. "Someone stole my grandmother."

Betty's eyebrows rose up to meet her curls. "What, right out of her grave?"

"Right out of the ground, and in November, too. It had to be tough to dig her up."

"Goodness. That must be quite the shock." She blinked. "I don't think you've got any necromancers on your island at the moment, so you can rest easy there."

"Necromancers?" My voice came out weak and dough-nut-scented.

"They're annoying buggers, and they do love a good cemetery, but they're rare. The professionals, anyway. Every so often you come across an amateur who's seen *The*

Mummy a few times too many and the only thing he manages to raise is trouble. But your problem isn't necromancers, not if they swiped your grandma's coffin, too. They're only ever interested in the body itself, not the accouterments."

I seized on the part of that sentence that stuck out. "He?"

"Oh, yes. Necromancers tend to be men. Women have got better things to do than raise the dead, unless they've got a powerful broken heart. Then they can raise hell. No, your average necromancer falls into three categories." Betty ticked them off on her fingers. "A man who wants more power and thinks he can get it from the deceased; a man who fancies a harem of mindless sex slaves and isn't picky about the smell; or a man who wants an army he can boss around without having to open his wallet."

Another doughnut vanished while I listened. Somehow this one was as warm as the first one, and had that same perfect crackle and softness. There was magic in the Cake Emporium's kitchen—literally.

"So they're basically raising zombies?"

"A zombie eats brains for fuel. A reanimated corpse relies on the necromancer's magic to sustain itself. It takes a lot of energy to move a body when it doesn't have a soul behind the wheel."

"Zombies are real?" My voice was faint, distant.

"In a manner of speaking. You'll find most things are real. Our imaginations aren't quite that good." She patted my hand. "You'll find your grandma and your friend. You always do. In the meantime, ask your question. I know you've got one."

"Dozens," I admitted. "But the most immediate one is about spirit boards. Are they strictly for emailing ghosts, or can you reach out and touch something else?" I gave her a quick breakdown of the Konstantinos Grivas situation.

Betty made a face that bothered me. She shook her head. Curls danced about her cheeks. "Those things are trouble in the wrong hands. I know we sell them, but we're careful about who gets one. The thing about a spirit board is that you can contact anything that wants to be contacted. And the things that want to reach out aren't always nice. You found it under your dead man?"

"Under his caboose." I told her what Maria Griva had told me earlier.

"Dear me. A person can do a lot of damage with those things if they have a bit of talent and no know-how whatsoever. You tell your policeman that whatever that poor fool was trying to call, it wasn't necessarily a ghost. His wife might be right about devils."

————

On foot, I headed for home. While I was walking, I called Toula. Her disapproval wafted across the island before she even said hello.

"Everything okay?" I asked her.

"No, everything is not okay. My children are outside playing with dead people. At least that's what they told me."

"Did you tell them not to play with dead people?"

"I tried, but they said the dead people followed them inside. I don't want ghosts in my house!"

"A-ha! So you admit ghosts are real?"

"I admit nothing. Allie …" her voice dropped to a worried whisper "… what did I do wrong?"

"The same thing our parents did with me: nothing.

This isn't about anything you did or didn't do. Milos and Patra see ghosts."

"Do they need therapy? We can take them to therapy. What about medication? They have pills for everything now."

"Only if your penis won't go up and down like it used to."

She went silent. Toula disapproved of me using words like "penis" in a sentence.

"Should I have said 'dick'?" I asked. "Let's pretend I said that instead."

"Please tell me you called with good news. Are Mom and Dad coming home early?"

"Um …"

Her voice sharpened to a diamond hard point. "What?"

"Nothing."

"Just tell me."

"Someone dug up Yiayia's grave and stole her and her coffin."

There was a clinking in the background. "What is that?"

"Ouzo."

"So early?"

"So late," she said. "So very, very late. Screw it. My children can play with their ghosts. I'm going to drink and watch daytime TV until I pass out."

"Want me to watch the kids?"

"No, they've got a bunch of dead relatives watching out for them. Call me if you find Yiayia. Or don't."

On that ouzo-soaked note, she ended the call.

Poor Toula. She was going through things. But in her defense she was handling it pretty well for a complete basket case.

A car engine cut into my internal monologue. It gave a quick honk, then Leo pulled up alongside me. He buzzed down the window.

"Done at the cemetery?" I called out.

"I'm on my way to let Kyria Griva know her husband is dead."

I made a face. "Good luck with that."

"I could use a lucky charm."

"Too bad I'm all out of rabbits' feet. Although to be honest I doubt the veracity of those things. They're not lucky for the rabbit, are they?"

He looked at me. Meaningfully.

"No," I said.

"I'll give you anything."

"There's nothing I want."

He looked me up and down like *that*. "Really?"

Blood rushed to various body parts. My cheek flushed. There were things I wanted and I wanted them from Leo. Had we not been in public, where everything has ears and mouths, I might have told him. Instead, I settled for relatively benign.

"How about a back rub?"

"And put my hands all over you? Deal," he said without a second thought. "Come on. I want to notify the widow before she hears it from someone else. You know how this place is."

The odds weren't in his favor. Gossip on Merope moved at the speed of something scientists only wished they could harness. Load it into a spaceship's engine and mankind could land on Mars in under a minute.

I jumped in and we were off, racing against physics.

The Grivas family lived—well, not Konstantinos Grivas as of today—in an apartment building not too different to mine. Same three levels. Same white stucco that received a fresh slapping of whitewash this summer. Functioning shutters at every window.

In the courtyard, Maria Griva—as was customary, she lost the S on the end of her name because of her ovaries--was giving the concrete hell with her whiskbroom. A hose lay coiled near the faucet. Soon it would get its turn.

Long before Greeks were called Greeks, they stood outside their homes and shooed dust and debris away with twigs. Why, probably I'd never know. To keep bad spirits away maybe. Ghosts didn't care. They stepped right over brooms. Or maybe it was an excuse to be outside, where Greeks could keep both eyes on the neighborhood. One never knew when hot gossip would happen. Best to be outside to catch it.

Maria Griva's head jerked up as Leo stopped at the curb. We got out. Her gaze immediately zeroed in on me.

"You! Where is my husband, eh? Go find him!"

In a way, I already had. But I wasn't sure she'd appreciate the circumstances or the result.

Further down the street, an impending storm hustled toward us. A pair of old crows shrouded in black dresses, knee-high stockings, and black shawls, their steel gray hair partially hidden under black kerchiefs. Faces hard, determined. Their cheeks, normally hollow and ravaged by time and an overabundance of salt air and relentless sunshine, bulged with barely restrained gossip.

"Talk fast," I told Leo. "We're about to have company."

One of the women bent down to remove one of her two slip-on shoes.

"Kyria Griva," Leo said, "I regret to inform you—"

The black slipper sailed through the air.

Smack.

Leo went down. As he fell, he dragged me with him, sheltering me with his body.

"Slipper," I said breathlessly. "Not bullets."

Back home they'd call it "assaulting a law enforcement officer." Here flying slippers meant you were in trouble. Leo was nanoseconds away from scooping the biddies. Let a policeman snatch their headline? Never.

Leo opened his mouth.

I clapped my hand over it. "Think carefully. Do you want war with Merope's old women? You might need them for other cases. This is your reputation and career on the line."

"Maria, your Konstatinos is dead!" one of them hollered in her loudest outside voice.

The other one was full of helpful news, too. "The police found him naked in the cemetery with a spirit board stuck to his *kolos*!"

Maria Griva kicked off her own shoe. She dropped her broom, picked up the slip-on footwear, and rushed at us.

"Uh oh," I said. "Nothing good is about to happen."

"I have a gun," Leo said. "I was hoping they would respect that."

"You must be kidding."

Konstantinos Grivas' widow rained blows on Leo's back. Good thing he was wearing a padded coat. "Why did you not tell me, eh? That is your job!"

He looked at me. "I tried."

"I know," I said. "You really did." There were only a few meters between us and protective cover. "We should crawl."

The slipper kept on coming. Leo was doing his best to shelter me from the worst. "I don't think I can make it."

I rolled onto my back and dug around in my bag. Pepper spray was a constant presence in my bag, just in case, but my reputation would die faster than a salted slug if I pepper sprayed a respected—well, an elderly member of the community. People talked, and they loved to talk about young people today and how they didn't respect their elders.

What else did I have?

A saltshaker, old receipts, and lip balm. Nothing to defeat a trio of attacking widows.

"We should just make a run for it," I said. "We can do this. It's just slippers."

On that note, Maria Griva remembered the broom she'd been holding before the gossip struck. She shuffled to snatch up the broom.

"Now," Leo said. He dragged me up off the ground and we ran for our lives, broom snapping at our heels.

CHAPTER FIVE

IN THE END, Leo lost the passenger side mirror when Maria Griva struck it with the broom handle. But we were safe, that's all that mattered.

We sat on the front step outside our apartment building, panting. Nearby, Yiannis the dead gardener was raking leaves. He waved, and I waved back while pretending to fiddle with my hair.

"I thought we were going to die—well, mostly you," I said.

Leo faked shock. "You would have let me die by slipper?"

In Greece all kids grow up fearing the flying *pandofla*— slipper. The *Pandofla* of Judgment and Punishment can come out of nowhere at any time, and the hand wielding them is always expert. But Leo was safe. I'd lost one man to a heart condition. I wouldn't lose this one to footwear.

"Do people usually react that way when you give them bad news?"

"People are predictable until they're not. Grief twists people into strange shapes, and who they are is not always who you'll see when they hear the worst news imaginable. This isn't the first time I've been attacked on the job. It's the first time a broom was involved, though."

He was right and I knew it. When Andreas died I wasn't Allie Callas for the longest time. Eventually I'd rediscovered myself, and now I was sitting on a step, dying to make out with Leo.

"I don't suppose anyone's located my grandmother yet?"

"Not yet," he said. "We don't have anything. Did you get anything on the spirit board?"

I indicated that I had. "The bad news is that you can call up anything with a pair of willing ears, not just ghosts."

"What kind of anything?"

"Demons. Other assorted oogie boogies."

Leo blew out a sigh that said he couldn't believe he was taking this seriously. His phone buzzed. He glanced at the screen. "Got to go," he said. "Crime never takes a break."

"It's not my grandmother, is it?"

"Someone called in claiming Crusty Dimitri's is a crime scene."

"Isn't that everyone who's ever been there?"

Crusty Dimitri's is a local eatery that delivers food-like substances that may or may not contain actual food. Its food substance has, on occasion, contained such ingredients as cockroaches and stray bits of plastic. Nobody who lives on the island eats there if they can help it. Unfortunately, it's the only place that delivers when you're drinking at home alone and all bad ideas suddenly sound good. You'd think the place would get shut down for health violations, and you'd be right if Crusty Dimitri's was located anywhere else. Except the owner's brother is Merope's health inspector. They don't have to exchange money, just plans for their aged parents' care.

Leo kissed me—twice and hard—then he was gone.

What a day, and it wasn't even noon yet. I was several bruises richer, so that was something, right?

Pathetic and downtrodden, I climbed the stairs with my backpack. Angela was still missing, and now Yiayia was unaccounted for, along with her coffin. I let myself into my apartment and flopped down on my office chair. My laptop came to life instantly. First things first, I ran a search to see if anyone had encountered a decaying coffin with an equally decrepit old woman.

The answer was yes, but not in this country and definitely not on Merope. Otherwise, it was a big fat no.

"Computers! Ha! Machines tell you nothing. You want to know things, talk to people," a male voice said behind me.

Konstantinos Grivas. Recently deceased. And he was peering over my shoulder. Naked.

For crying out loud. Why me?

From the neck down he was plucked poultry. A loose skinned turkey. A half starved chicken. I did my best to keep my eyes above the waist and away from the dangling bird neck. His head was mostly nose and ears.

Virgin Mary. Another freakin' ghost in my apartment.

"Murdered?" I asked him. "Or are you on some other mission like your friend in my bathroom?"

"I know nothing," he said. His face said he knew all kinds of things.

"Well, I have questions and the police do, too," I said.

"Tell her nothing," Yiorgos Dakis said from my bathroom.

"How about you tell me everything," I said. "Let's start with the spirit board."

The ghost of Konstantinos Grivas scowled. "He said it would work. Why it did not work, I do not know."

"Because you are incompetent," came the voice from the bathroom.

"Says the *malakas* hiding in a bathroom," Grivas said.

"Were you watching me at the cemetery, *re, pousti*?"

"Wait," I said. "We? He? Can we put some names on these people?"

"He never told me his name, the man who gave me the spirit board," Grivas said. "Only that it would get me what I wanted."

"What did you want?"

"To talk to your grandmother, of course."

My mind reeled, boggled, and a few other verbs that suggested a sudden lack of equilibrium. "My grandmother? Why?"

"*Skasmos!*" said the toilet-bound ghost.

"Don't shut up. Ignore him," I said. "He's powerless."

"She trapped me on the toilet!" Dakis yelled.

"And you could leave right now if you promise to go away forever." Back to Grivas. "Did you have something to do with Yiayia's empty grave?"

"What?" the man in the bathroom barked. "Let me out of here! I want to participate in this conversation."

"Participate from there," I told him.

"Let me out!" he yelled.

"You want out? You have to earn it."

"The Virgin Mary's *mouni*," Yiorgos Dakis swore.

"What do you want?" Konstantinos Grivas asked sulkily.

"Information," I said.

"I cannot give you that," he said in a tone that sounded scared. "If I do, they might hurt me."

I hated to point out the obvious. Death can be a sore

subject for some ghosts. But under the circumstances I was happy to make an exception.

"You're dead. Nothing can hurt you." Was that true, though? Roger Wilson, ghost tormentor and jailer, was dead when a giant swirling hole opened in the ceiling and sucked up his spirit. "Almost nothing."

"That is what you think," Dakis said from the toilet.

"They could call us back," Konstantinos Grivas said. "At any time, if they have got a functioning spirit board."

A stream of obscenities shot out of my bathroom. "Stop talking, *vre*! *Skatofatsa* salt. Being a ghost is the worst. I cannot touch anything!"

Salt didn't have a face; so calling it a "poop face" was inaccurate, if not colorful.

I leaned against the bathroom's doorframe. Dakis had at least pulled up his underwear.

"I'll let you off the toilet, but you have to answer my questions."

Yiorgos Dakis considered it for a moment. "Okay."

"Deal?"

"I said okay."

With the tip of my boot, I broke the salt line.

Yiorgos Dakis chopped his groin with both hands, a gesture inviting me to partake of his old, withered, and very dead genitals. Then, with a loud *pop*, he vanished.

Fabulous. Just fabulous. So much for our deal.

There was another *pop*, this time from the living room. I darted in just time to see Yiorgos Dakis grab Konstantinos Grivas by the elbow. With a third *pop*, they exited the building.

Then I was alone.

For once, when I didn't want to be.

———

When the going got tough, I made lists. Not for Santa—I was beyond sitting on his lap. For myself.

Who gave Konstantinos Grivas the spirit board?

Why did he want to talk to my grandmother?

Who else was in on all this weirdness?

(I needed names, darn it.)

Where was Angela, and was she okay?

And where was Yiayia?

I took my problems across the street to Merope's Best, which sells Merope's worst coffee, served by sullen baristas in sardonic t-shirts that often make sense in no language whatsoever. Case in point, the Fack the Fack shirt currently clinging to a wiry teenager in last night's makeup or this morning's artful smokey eye. I couldn't tell the difference.

"Want to try the special?" she asked me.

"Should I?"

"Who cares?"

Today's special was a baklava latte. Sounded like heaven in a paper cup. Knowing Merope's Best they'd find a way to screw it up.

I ordered it anyway.

While I waited for the barista to work up the will to make the thing, I eyed the clientele. A couple of tables were already occupied by the dead, who, for whatever, reason loved the joint. Probably this was where they'd died, choking on burnt beans or undeclared peanuts. The rest were teenagers and other assorted people with terrible taste. But who was I to judge them? I was here, wasn't I?

"Alfie," the barista said. She shoved a paper cup across the counter with one black-tipped finger. I took it. I was Alfie.

The coffee wasn't half bad, but the half that wasn't bad wasn't good. I drank it anyway, out of desperation mostly. Something to kick start my brain and keep at least one of my hands warm. One-handed, I rode back out to the cemetery, thoughts churning. Leo and Pappas had cordoned off my grandmother's empty grave with yellow tape. There was more of the same around the spot where Pappas had almost puked on Konstantinos Grivas's body.

Stuck on stupid, I started down into Yiayia's grave, trying to will the universe to spit out answers. The universe remained tight-lipped. Wherever answers were going to come from, it wasn't here.

"Fools," a man's voice said behind me. "A body is not who we are. It is merely a puppet for the soul."

I knew that rich, melodious, and vaguely British voice. The man attached—if that's what he was—sounded as though he belonged in an old library, poring over fantastic maps and devouring forbidden tomes. "Like the little alien guy in Men in Black?"

The Man in Black ignored my clever pop culture reference. He stood beside me. "You are wondering, of course, why your grandmother's remains were stolen."

"At the moment I'm less interested in the *why* and more concerned with the *where* and the *who*. After that I'll worry about *why*. I'm sure it can't be anything good or not-weird. Sane people don't abduct bodies."

"They are attempting to fulfill a promise."

"Who is 'they' and where did 'they' take my grandmother?"

"When you understand the promise, you will know where she is."

"Or, you could just save me time and tell me. There's somewhere else I need to be, and time isn't exactly on my side—or maybe it's nothing, I don't know. I don't know much right now, and I don't like it."

"All children must learn to walk, eventually," he said, not at all cryptically.

"I can walk. What I can't do is find one decaying coffin with my grandmother inside."

"You can find anything, Miss Callas. That is your gift."

"My gift? What about seeing ghosts?"

"Anyone can see the dead if they wish it hard enough. But being able to find the improbable, the impossible, the lost and hidden is a rare skill. People compensate you for finding those things that make their lives better and happier, and for good reason. Not everybody can find what is missing from their lives, even when those objects are right in front of them."

"So you're saying finding things is my gift?"

"It has always come easily to you, has it not?"

"Because I work at it, and I have access to technology that makes finding needles in haystacks easier." Plus I had Sam, who could reach out and snatch information out of the virtual word with a few seductive keystrokes."

"You underestimate yourself, Miss Callas."

He turned around. I watched him walk away, all mood and mist. I half expected him to disappear the way ghosts do. But he kept on going, visible the same as any regular person, until he reached the road.

CHAPTER SIX

I CALLED LEO.

"Any leads about Yiayia's body?"

"You asked me that not even an hour ago."

"I'm desperate."

"None," he said. "But she hasn't been missing long."

"Merope isn't big. No one can pass gas without the rest of the island knowing. A decrepit coffin is unusual, even for here. Someone had to see it."

And I was right. Everyone on the island saw everything. Secrets never stayed secrets for long, unless they were too small for anyone to care about. Even then, someone always knew. Usually me. People like telling me things. I've got one of those faces, I guess. Plus people like passing on information. There's no secret that burns brighter than someone else's secret.

"I've got nothing yet, Allie. As soon as I know something, you'll know, too."

"Are you going to investigate?"

He went quiet.

"What is it?" I asked him.

"Someone in the department will look into it …"

"Pappas," I said. "You mean Pappas, right?"

"Pappas is a good cop, and he's better suited for theft than homicide."

"Homicide?"

In my haste to squeeze information out of Konstantinos Grivas, I'd forgotten to grill him about how he'd met his maker (although he probably hadn't technically "met" her or him or it yet, if there was such a being or thing) after my initial question. Given his proximity to Yiayia's grave and the spirit board stuck to his behind, I'd assumed weird fetish gone wrong. Yiorgos Dakis and his death-by-spanking-the-mortadella while tugging on a stocking and wearing his underpants as a gimp mask had clouded my judgment. Now every dead man associated with Yiayia was a sexual deviant, in my mind.

"Panos says Grivas bled out from two stab wounds in his neck."

"I didn't see any blood," I said, "or any stab wounds, but then there were a lot of bushes. Constable Pappas's vomit clouded the issue, too."

"Hasn't rained much either, so the dirt soaked up most of the blood before it could make a big mess. As soon as we rolled him over we saw the holes."

I winced. "How long had he been … gone?"

"Estimated time of death, sometime between 3:00 AM and dawn."

"So someone stabbed him and dumped him in the bushes?"

"More likely they stabbed him in the bushes and left him there. There were no signs of blood anywhere else, and no evidence that he'd been dragged into the bushes. Pappas doesn't have the stomach for homicide yet, which is why I'm putting him on your grandmother's case."

"What if the person who killed Grivas stole Yiayia?"

"Then we will know soon enough. Right now we're treating them as separate crimes. If they're connected hopefully that will make things easier."

I didn't tell him about the Man in Black's strange message about fulfilling promises. Not that it didn't seem pertinent—it kind of was—but in an unhelpful way that was likely to get me locked up for twenty-four hours observation. The Man in Black didn't seem to exist. Oh, he was solid enough; definitely not a ghost, but he had the permanence of mist. He came and went, often after I was injured, and dispensed the kind of advice a well-meaning relative without any grip on reality would give. That's not the kind of thing you take to the police, not even one you make out with on a regular basis.

"What are you doing tonight?" Leo asked me.

"That depends on whether or not you're going to make good on that back rub."

"That's the plan," he said. "I hope you can handle it."

"I can handle a lot."

"Good thing I've got plenty for you to handle."

"Now you're just bragging," I said.

"It's not bragging if it's accurate."

I told him I had to go, which was true, in a sense. The Northern Hemisphere was veering toward winter, but things were heating up in my jeans. There were limits to what I could handle in the middle of the street. Alone. With loads of witnesses.

Witnesses.

All these people and no one saw a person, persons, or donkey hauling my grandmother's casket around?

As Ralph Wiggins once said: Unpossible!

Every small community consists of dispersal nodes. Hubs that gossip passes through before fanning out to other parts of society. One of Merope's nodes was close by. That was my next stop.

The More Super Market isn't super—or more super than the Super Super Market—but it's definitely a market. It sells groceries. Ergo: market. The Super Super Market sits closer to my apartment on a map, but my fiancé never dropped dead in the More Super Market. Therefore, I take my business to the market that doesn't fill me with horror and sadness when I need basics like salami and cheese.

Greece isn't a country of supermarkets, although some are making inroads on the mainland. But the likes of Lidl haven't reached Merope; so shopping remains compartmentalized. We have meat shops (never call it a butcher or people will think you're shopping for penis), and bakeries, and produce stores, and little markets that fill the gaps. Little markets like the More Super Market, which was formerly owned by the slightly homicidal Triantafillou brothers and currently owned by nobody knew whom.

Regardless of who was handing out paychecks, the omnipresent cashier was Stephanie Dolas, a high school dropout, barely in her twenties. Stephanie suffers from over-plucked eyebrows that she draws back on daily with a thick, black pencil. Her makeup always says, "When I grow up I want to be a botanical garden or a tropical aviary." Stephanie Dolas know things. And the reason she knows things is that sooner or later, most of the island's denizens filter through the More Super Market. When they do, they gossip with their neighbors, friends, and adversaries. Stephanie's ears are there to catch it all. Her mouth lobs it to the next available ear.

Often that ear is mine.

I rode to the More Super Market, cobbling a short shopping list in my head. When I got there, Stephanie was plucking her mustache. I ordered a chunk of feta at the deli, a smaller, more expensive chunk of kaseri cheese, and carried them to the checkout with a half-kilo of salami.

Stephanie kept on plucking the dark, rebellious hairs, one at a time.

"They have wax for that," I pointed out. "And cream that basically dissolves the hair."

"Plucking relaxes me."

She shook the tweezers. A hair landed on my cheese's brown paper wrapper. I blew it away.

"What's new?" I asked the distracted cashier.

"I heard Kyrios Dakis was found dead on your grandmother's grave."

"True story," I said.

Surprised, she quit plucking for a moment. I didn't make a habit of confirming or denying rumors. Today I was happy to do some give and take. I was floundering.

"Really?"

"Really."

"Was it a weird sex thing?"

"Sex implies a partner. Kyrios Dakis was alone."

She thought about that a moment. "Oh. Oh-h-h-h-h."

"Oh," I agreed.

Since I was apparently in a giving mood, she hit me with a question. "And is it true that Kyrios Grivas was found in the bushes in the graveyard, too?"

"Naked, and with a spirit board under his *kolos*. I don't suppose you've heard anyone mention a stolen coffin with, say, a dead woman inside."

"What woman?"

"My grandmother."

Plucking resumed. "No. I am sure I would remember that."

"Most people would, I think."

A wet, heavy blanket draped over my shoulders,

metaphorically speaking. A dead end. Moving a coffin and a grandmother requires strength, transportation, equipment. Two of those things invoke questions and speculation and gossip.

Since there was no gossip, whoever stole Yiayia must have concealed the maneuver as normal activity. There was nothing more normal at a cemetery than the comings and goings of the cemetery's caretaker.

I texted Leo.

—*Did you talk to the cemetery caretaker?*

—*Not yet.*

I perked up. It wasn't all doom and gloom. Finding things was my jam, right? The Man in Black said so. I could find Yiayia's body thief.

With the cheese and salami in my bicycle's basket, I rode off in search of the local cemetery's caretaker. Given that the current ambient temperature was racing my refrigerator to barely above freezing, my deli goods were safe in my bicycle's basket.

Recent spate of murders aside, people don't die all that often on Merope. The Mediterranean diet keeps folks going long past the rest of the world's use-by date. And when they expire, their families—the ones who'd escaped to the mainland to pursue careers—have their remains shipped elsewhere for burial. That saves the families from sailing to Merope to pay their yearly respects. So the island employs one man to keep the graves weeded and the plots organized. That one man used to be a kid in my high school class.

I found Christos Fekkas honing the edge of a gleaming shovel, outside the house where he lives with his mother. He isn't one of life's basement dwellers because houses on Merope don't have basements. His mother's house does have a screened porch. Christos sleeps there during the warmer months. In winter his mother lets him sleep on the kitchen floor, near the wood-burning oven where she cooks their meals.

Smoke curled up and away from the crooked chimney. The air smelled like spices hiding a terrible secret. The secret in this case was that whatever Kyria Fekka was cooking, it should have been cast into the garbage several days ago. I did my best to breathe and speak through the same air hole.

Christos Fekkas was the smartest kid in school. He was going places, or so the teachers used to tell us all, to motivate and mock us. In the end the only place he went was nowhere. Instead of pursuing a university education, he performed his mandatory national service, then applied to the local government for the cemetery caretaker job, which they gave him on account of how the previous one died in a freak fishing accident. The man reeled in his fish, unhooked his fish, and the fish spat the bait and hook back at him. His mouth was open at the time and that hook caught in his throat. The bait blocked the airway. And that was the end of his career as the cemetery's caretaker.

So Christos and his high IQ walked right in to an open position. Since then he'd been digging graves and weeding to the best of any caretaker's abilities.

"Allie." Christos kept on honing. "Nobody in your family died recently, did they?"

Christos Fekkas doesn't look like he watches over dead folks for a living. He's got the body of a gym rat and the head of whichever Olympian god had thick, luxurious black hair. He's single, but according to the local buzz it's because he always smells like dirt.

"Not today," I said.

"Did you want to purchase a plot for yourself?" he said. "Not for today, but … eventually?"

"My plan is to live forever. So far it's working out pretty well." I nodded to the tools in his hands. "New shovel?"

"Old shovel. That's why I'm not at the cemetery yet, because I want to finish this first. I like to keep my tools sharp and polished for when I break new ground. It's a thing I do. I always start a grave by hand. Seems more personal that way."

That wasn't weird at all. "Lose any bodies lately?"

"Never on my watch." His forehead scrunched up. "Why?"

Wow. Somehow I'd managed to beat the local gossips *and* the police to the scoop. I watched Christos carefully as I brought him up to date about Yiayia's clandestine exit from her hole in the ground and Konstantinos Grivas's murder in the cemetery's bushes.

He set aside the shovel and stood abruptly. "I have to go," he said. "The police will want to speak to me."

Jumpy or diligent?

My money was on diligent. The Christos Fekkas I knew was an okay guy. Not the kind to stick his fingers in his ears and go "la-la-la" if someone offered him a few euro to look the other way while they excavated a grave.

"There's not much you can do now."

"I thought this would happen," he said, "so I set up a camera in case the police needed evidence."

"What would happen? Body theft?"

"Your grandmother in particular."

"Why?"

"There was unusual activity."

"Like scores of visitors?"

He indicated *yes*. "They tried to buy your grandmother's body."

"Who? When?"

"Her friends. Maybe a month ago they offered me a lot

of money and extra for the use of my equipment so they could move her to a different location. Nobody uses my equipment except me, and nobody digs up one of my clients unless they have got an exhumation order signed by the authorities. They shunned Mama when I told them no."

Shunning? Did we even do that? Were we Amish?

Worse. We were Greek. Greek shunning makes the Amish look like shunning amateurs. When Greeks shun you, you get shunned good and hard.

Don't want to play by the island's rules?

Shun.

Forget to greet someone or ignore a wave?

Shun.

The grey-haired set from my grandmother's generation was spoiled. They scored respect and capitulation by default thanks to their ages (ages they lied about because Greek women from past generations would fall on a sword before admitting to the real birth year on their identification) and connections to the past. The generation below me was learning to dispense merit-based respect. You want respect? Earn it. To the next generation, the only thing old age meant was that so far you had avoided death.

Anyway, Merope's elders—or a certain subset—had made a demand and been rebuffed. Naturally they turned up the frost. Social shunning was the one tool they possessed since they couldn't slap Fekkas's mother with a *pandofla* or whack her with the wooden spoon.

Boy, if you asked me they were playing a risky game messing with the mother of the man who buried their bodies.

"Who, specifically?"

He offered up two names: Yiorgos Dakis and Konstantinos Grivas. Both dead. "They mentioned others," he said. "But they did not give names."

"Can I see the video footage, if it caught anything?"

"Come."

Christos didn't have a car. But the good news was that he owned a motorcycle leftover from one of the old World Wars. Probably the first one. I could have ridden my bicycle, told him I'd meet him there instead of climbing on back of his spluttering death machine, but I was a woman without a ton of spare time. If the camera caught anything useful, my grandmother might be back in her grave where she belonged in hours. Then I could race through Betty's portal to the UK to find Angela.

"Hold on tight," Christos said. "Sometimes it brakes without warning."

Oh, goodie.

For the next couple of minutes Christos swerved and dodged livestock and the random rocks that inevitably found their way onto Merope's dirt roads. Nature didn't make these roads; nature wanted its land back. When nature didn't get its way, it hurled rocks at the roads.

When we stopped at the onsite caretaker's workshop, I asked the question that had been rattling around my back of my mind for years. "Why the cemetery? You had your pick of any career."

"I like dead people," Christos Fekkas said. "They are uncomplicated."

Uncomplicated? He had no idea.

The workshop door was unlocked. That was Merope for you. Locals didn't steal from each other—that was considered bad manners—so most of the time doors went unlocked and windows remained open during the summer months.

The workshop contained a desk and filing cabinet, a

small backhoe and accessories, tarps, a variety of shovels, spades, clippers, and other yard work staples. Everything shone, from the floor to the smallest pair of shears. Christos was a cemetery caretaker and gravedigger, but he was the best caretaker and gravedigger, darn it. He took pride in burying the dead.

In one of the desk's drawers—it was locked—he retrieved a tablet. He tapped a few times, held the device between us.

"This only records when there is motion." He scrolled. There was Pappas arriving at the scene of what was about to be called a crime. Minutes later, Leo and I showed up.

"Not a lot of entries," I said.

"People like to talk about how they loved the deceased. But when it comes to visiting they are always too busy. Only one man comes every day."

"Let me guess. Is it Kyrios Psaris?"

"Yes."

Stavros Psaris lost his son, his wife, and then his last love, my best friend and neighbor Olga Marouli. He never got over any of them. The gentle retired lawyer and I had something in common besides our affection for Olga. Like me, he could see ghosts.

The relatively new but familiar ache flared in my chest. The next couple of breaths hurt before returning to their usual painless selves. I missed Olga and our friendship every day.

"Konstantinos Grivas was likely killed during the night, and that's probably when Yiayia was stolen, too."

Christos tapped again. The screen came to life. Thugs descended on the cemetery. Elderly bandits who didn't waste time on discretion. They did what they wanted, took what they wanted. First they rolled out the backhoe, and then they got to work hauling Yiayia and her coffin out of the ground. There was no sound or we'd have heard them complaining about their legs and feet. (But we wouldn't know if the pain was in their legs or feet, seeing as how the Greek word for both body parts is the same: *podia*.)

When the senior citizens were done, someone parked the backhoe back in its place while the others played pallbearers and carried the coffin away on foot.

This whole time, Christos had been opening and closing his mouth like a fish. Finally, he found words. "They can't do that!"

"And yet, they did. They dug her up and bolted. Who knew they had it in them?"

Modern technology was no slouch. The faces weren't crystal clear—it was the middle of the night—but good enough to identify every last thief. They were all senior citizens. There wasn't an original hip among them.

They were Yiayia's friends. Minus Dakis and Grivas.

"What about the murder?" I said. "Is there another other recording from this morning?"

He tapped. New entry, new timestamp just minutes before the old folks made off with my grandmother.

Konstantinos Grivas approached Yiayia's grave. On old and creaking knees, he crouched down and set up the spirit board. Before he had a chance to place his finger on the doodad, his head jerked up. He picked up the board, tucked it under his arm, and set off in the direction of the bushes. Which conveniently happened to be just beyond the camera's eye.

He was fully dressed, I noticed. Somewhere along the way he'd lost his clothes.

"You need to give this to Leo—Detective Samaras."

Christos raised both eyebrows. "I heard you were dating. Is that still on? Isn't it weird? Because he used to date your sister when we were in high school, right?"

"Yeah, it's weird."

"But not weird enough to stop?"

"Not weird enough to stop."

"But not not-weird enough to go fully public?"

"Exactly."

He tapped the screen and ran the footage again. Konstantinos Grivas disappeared into the bushes once more. The next time I saw him he was dead. The time after that he was a ghost in my apartment.

My phone bing-bonged.

—*Were you riding on a motorcycle with Christos Fekkas?*

The power of gossip had compelled Toula to text me.

—*Maybe. Why?*

—*What about Leo?*

—*The ride was business, not pleasure.*

The phone went silent. My sister was judging me. Her conflicting emotions wafted across the island. Riding on the motorcycle with Christos wasn't proper in her mind. Not because motorcycles are bad but because it was a slow news day and suddenly there I was, gallivanting around Merope with Christos Fekkas. And also because I was dating Leo. But if I was riding around with another guy who wasn't Leo, then was she supposed to be happy or sad it was over?

It wasn't easy being Toula. My sister put on a respectable face, but on the inside she was a mess.

My phone bing-bonged again. Not Toula this time. Leo.

—*Were you just riding on a motorcycle with Christos Fekkas?*

—*Business, not pleasure.*

—*I figured. Did he have anything useful?*

—*Does video count?*

—*Of Grivas' murder?*

—*Sort of. But mostly grave-robbing.*

—We'll be right there.

If Leo was bothered by me bopping around the island behind Fekkas, it didn't show. I was relieved. That meant he wasn't about to kowtow to the island's gossipmongers.

"The police are on their way," I told Christos.

While we were waiting, I wandered over to where Pappas had discovered Grivas' body. "At least he didn't kill himself by accident like Yiorgos Dakis," I said.

Christos pinkened. By the time he reached full blush his face looked like a pot of geraniums in bloom.

"I've seen weird things," he said. "But never that."

"What's the weirdest thing you've seen, besides Dakis' surprise unhappy ending?"

"You would never believe me."

I opened my mouth to tell him that I tended to believe at least ten crazy things before breakfast. It was too late. His phone rang. He took off to answer it. Which left me alone to wait for the police.

Ten minutes later, Constable Pappas showed up, minus Leo.

"Are there bodies?" he asked me.

"Not any fresh ones," I told him.

"Good enough. Detective Samaras said you have something for me."

I handed him the iPad, showed him the Yiayia heist, followed by the second to last moments of Grivas' life.

"I'll send this to Detective Samaras," he said about the second clip. That made sense since Leo was working the homicide. "What about these people stealing the … your grandmother? Do you know them?"

"I do, and you do, too." I reeled off a string of names.

Pappas knew them all by name and reputation, even if he'd never spoken to them beyond a wave and a brief interrogation about his family.

"I will talk to them," he said.

He stood there. He did a whole lot of nothing.

"Now?" I said. "They're all retired. They should be home, sweeping their yards and minding their neighbors' business. Except the men, and you'll most likely find them in one *kafeneio* or another at this time of day."

My bet was a safe one. Retired Greek men flocked to the coffee shops during the day to meet with their peers—their peers being other old men who enjoyed yelling about politics and playing backgammon while they complained about their wives. Wives they'd never leave because then who would cook their lunch and wash their underpants?

Pappas didn't move a muscle. The twitching eye didn't count, seeing as how it was involuntary.

I poked his forehead. "Are you paralyzed?"

"Ungh."

"Then what's the problem?"

"Those people, they are …"

"Old? Judgmental? Grave robbers?"

"Yes."

"Relax, you're a policeman. You've got the law on your side."

He shivered. "They scare me."

I waved vaguely at his belt. "You have a small gun and a big stick. If they're a problem, shoot at them or whack them with the stick."

"Have you seen what old women can do with a *pandofla?*"

I winced. I knew all about *pandoflas*. Case in point: this morning's run-in with Maria Griva. "Maybe you could call for backup."

Pappas looked at me. Hard. The meaning of that look wasn't lost on me. The young constable wanted me to tag along in case Merope's seniors attacked him with footwear.

"I'm not backup. I find things. I can find you backup if you want, but I'm not it."

"You could be backup."

"No."

"Please? What if they hurt me?"

"Fine," I said like he was killing me. Maybe it wouldn't be so bad. Those people stole my grandmother and the box she was buried in, so squeezing them for information might be fun, provided none of them had heart conditions. "Who's first?"

He scanned the list of names. "I don't know. They all scare me."

"Start with the weakest," I said. "They're easier to intimidate."

"Do we have to?"

"Normally I'd say no, that it's unkind to intimidate anyone, especially the elderly. But in this case we have them on camera, digging up a coffin."

"Do you think they're necrophiliacs?"

He sounded hopeful. Too hopeful.

"Pappas," I said. "You have issues."

"I really do."

CHAPTER SEVEN

Two MOTORCYCLE RIDES in one day. How long would it take Toula to nag me about this one?

My bicycle was still propped up outside the Fekkas house. Eventually I'd have to go back for it. Hopefully the Fekkases would be done with their meal by then. The smell had almost knocked me off my feet.

Our first stop was Kyrios—Mister—Papayiannis' house. He owns a cottage not far from my apartment. The way Yiayia used to tell it, she and Kyrios Papayiannis went on a couple of chaperoned dates before she married my long deceased grandfather. He never got over my grandmother, not even after he married his wife. Once his wife passed, he decided to take another shot at my grandmother. By then they had dead spouses in common. He courted Yiayia with flowers, cakes, little gifts. Maybe she gave him things in return, but my brain didn't want to know about them if she did. Papayiannis is a tiny scrap of a man, half my grandmother's size—and she wasn't a big woman. He was also the lead pallbearer in Yiayia's reverse burial.

We stood at the gate, the way Greeks do, and I called out to Kyrios Papayiannis because the man next to me, the one with the gun and the nightstick, had a chicken feather in his DNA.

Silence.

Nothing from the man who owned the white cracker box with the flaking blue shutters. His neighbors were super interested. Their necks craned. Their eyes opened. They eyed their phones. Easy to understand. Here I was, the island's find-it woman, shoulder to shoulder with a policeman. They were interested—and informative. The first to spill beans was Kyria Christina, a widow whose favorite hobbies were sweeping her yard and minding other people's business. Her devotion to her causes was admirable and helpful.

"He left in the middle of the night and he has not come home yet." She tacked on a disapproving noise. Men from good families did not venture out during the night, unless they were going fishing.

"Maybe he went fishing," I said.

"Maybe."

Her tone said no—no fishing for Papayiannis.

"Is this normal for him?" I asked.

"No." She eyed Pappas. "What is your family doing?" she asked him.

"They are good, Kyria Christina."

Her attention swung back to me. "Why are you looking for him, eh? Did he do a crime?"

She'd be salivating if she knew he'd helped rob a grave and a grandmother.

"He's writing a book and he asked me to help him find a policeman to interview. Voila!" I gestured at Constable Pappas. "A policeman."

She didn't look convinced. "A book?"

"A book," I said. "I think it must be a crime novel, don't you?"

"I did not know he could read."

Pappas chose that moment to find his voice. "Maybe he cannot read but he can write."

There was no logic in his logic, but that didn't slow me down. "Exactly," I said. "You never know with people." I glanced at my phone. "Would you look at the time? I have an appointment. If Kyrios Papayiannis shows up, do you think you could let me know?"

She was on the verge of asking why I cared, when I leaned closer to seal the deal. I glanced left, then right, then said, "But don't tell him you're calling me, okay? It's a secret."

On the one hand it was obvious her neighbor was involved in something dodgy. On the other, I was recruiting her as an informant. There was nothing locals loved more than being informants. World War II never really came to Merope.

She touched a finger to her eye. "I will call you when he comes home. I will say nothing. At least not to him."

We said our respectful goodbyes and rushed to the next name on the list.

Eugenia Droulia. Yiayia's best friend and worst enemy. In their generation it was the same thing. Frenemy before the word became popular.

Eugenia Droulia lives in a bungalow overlooking the water—which is all houses on the edge of the island. Her house is little more than a pile of stones, cobbled together with willpower and whitewash. During the summer, she rents out her garden shed to desperate tourists who can't squeeze into local hotels. For their euros they get a roof and the stink-eye from their temporary landlady. That's if she likes them. Eugenia Droulia is a small woman, vertically and horizontally. Most of her generation's women were raised by poor nutrition, and now their bones had thrown up their hands and gone "We're done holding up this biddy. Gravity can have her." She wears a kerchief that covers iron gray hair—hair that she perms periodically to remind it who's the boss, and she walks through life as though she detests the ground beneath her feet.

She liked me when I didn't speak or breathe.

All was quiet at Eugenia Droulia's home. Normally at this time of day she'd be out in her yard, judging her neighbors, minding their business, making up gossip as she swept the yard or fiddling with her potted garden. Today the yard was empty.

"Kyria Eugenia?" I called out.

"Maybe she is in the bathroom," Pappas said.

My gaze swiveled to the bathroom. The bathroom was a narrow outhouse at the back of the property. All flushing was accomplished via a bucket, filled at the pump in the front yard. The bucket was currently sitting next to the pump, empty. If Kyria Eugenia was in the bathroom, she'd been in too big a hurry to pump water.

"Maybe."

"You should go look," Pappas said like he wasn't the one with a badge and gun. "I will wait here, in case she shows up."

"If she's in there and she hits me with her slipper, I'm going to pass it on."

He thought about it for a moment. "I can live with that."

With my life in my hands, I eased through the gate and knocked on Eugenia Droulia's front door. No answer. I glanced back at Pappas. He mimed jiggling the handle. I opened the door. Peered in.

No sign of Kyria Eugenia. But she hadn't done her dishes.

The outhouse was more of the same. Wherever she was, it wasn't home.

On the surface it wasn't remotely weird that she was out at the same time as Kyrios Papayiannis. But just beneath my skin, where my suspicions like to crawl around, unfettered, bumping into each other and leaping to conclusions, nothing about this seemed okay or normal.

"They stole Yiayia and then they up and disappeared," I said to Pappas.

"What do you think that means?"

"Aren't you the policeman?"

"Yes, but I am not a good one."

"Yet," I said, trying to bolster his self-esteem.

He perked up. "Do you think I'll get better?"

"The more you do it, the better you'll get." I crossed my fingers in my pockets. "Same as learning anything."

"I will tell you what I think, if you tell me what you think."

"Okay, deal. What I think is that Yiayia's friends stole her body and now they're hiding out somewhere. Why, I don't know. They tried to buy her from the cemetery a month ago, so they obviously had plans." Horrible plans, most likely. Nobody stole an aged corpse for good.

"That is what I was thinking."

"Really?"

"No. I am still thinking necrophilia."

I blew out a sigh, scanned the list. "Let's try the next one."

We bumped across the island again to Merope's other edge, where Manolis Psaris owned a small vineyard. His grapes were adequate until he turned them into what could loosely be called wine. His wine was popular amongst people without taste buds--mostly his senior friends and unsuspecting tourists, who fell for the charm of small batch Greek wines. Psaris was Greek for *fish*, and Manolis Psaris played up the fish angle on his wine's labels. Stick figure Jesus turning water into wine. Manolis Psaris claimed his wine contained a secret ingredient. From the taste I guessed it was fish.

The Psaris property was hopping. A film crew was onsite, complete with a small trailer. Business must be good enough for Manolis Psaris to make a commercial. Huh. Who knew fishy wine was a moneymaker? A couple of cameramen had their cameras out, comparing features. A technological dick measuring in progress. There were women standing around in long robes, jiggling in the cold. And in the center of it all sat a handyman's workspace, complete with power tools, sawhorses, and wood.

As I climbed down off Pappas's motorcycle, a woman with an iPad in one hand hurried over. She looked mad at the world, the way I did before morning coffee.

"What is wrong with you?" she bellowed. "All those clothes. Get them off now or the camera will make it look like you've been whipped, along with the extra kilos it's going to add. Did you eat? Tell me you didn't eat in the last twenty-four hours. You'll get *kaka* everywhere." She looked me up and down, disapproving. "Of course you ate. I bet you can't help yourself. Nobody is a professional anymore."

I blinked in the thin light. Had I fallen into some bizarre hell dimension? Was that even a thing? Probably. These days, the impossible seemed to be possible, even probable.

"Is Kyrios Psaris here?"

She stopped. Her face scrunched up. "Who?"

"The man who owns this vineyard? The man you're making a commercial for?"

"Commercial!" She rolled her eyes and trotted off across the yard to the cluster of women in robes.

"I know her," Pappas said, gesturing at one of the women.

The woman in question was huddled with the others. She was somewhere between barely legal and middle age. Makeup was the culprit. Hair, too. She had too much of both. I was trying to guess the age of a woman hiding behind a Halloween mask of hair and cosmetics.

"Who is she?"

"Actress."

"What's she been in?"

He stared at me. I stared back. A piece was missing from this puzzle and I was starting to get the feeling I was the only one who couldn't stick it in the right place.

The young cop flushed. "Movies."

"What kind of movies? I like movies."

"Movies for adults."

My eye twitched. It knew what was up before the rest of me got a clue. "Action? Horror?"

Suddenly there was commotion as the trailer door slapped open. Out waddled a big voice with a tiny footprint.

"What are you doing here? Did you take a wrong turn on the way to your cave?"

Jimmy Kontos. Little person. *Nanos*. Adult film star. He struggled down the trailer steps in steel cap work boots, a tool belt made for a man two feet taller, and his birthday suit. He'd been manscaping and it showed.

I'd died and gone to hell, I just knew it.

"Tell me you're not filming one of your movies here," I said.

He hooked his thumbs in his tool belt. "*Tiny Men, Big Tools: Grapes of Wrath*."

"There's no grapes," I said. "It's almost winter."

"That's because they're wrath-ing."

Pappas' head swung left and right and back again. "What's it about?"

I thunked him on the forehead with my knuckle. "What do you think it's about?"

Jimmy beamed. "I'm glad you asked. This is the first one with a real and serious plot. It's about a man driven out of his home because of his insatiable sexual appetite and desire to build things. So he crosses the country, to find this vineyard in need of a man with a powerful hammer."

My eye twitched harder. "Can't you put some pants on?"

"Then I'd have to take them off again."

Pappas was staring at him.

Jimmy looked down. "What?"

"You're proportionate," Pappas said. "I wasn't sure dwarfs would be."

"It's shrinkage!"

"Kyrios Kontos?" someone called out. "The plow is ready."

"Got to go plow," Jimmy said, hurrying away. Sure enough, someone had a plow set up, complete with oxen to pull the load. "You should stay and watch."

The woman with the iPad approached again. "You are the one who finds things, yes?"

"That depends."

"Find us a goat. You will be well-compensated."

My eye twitch turned into an all-out flutter.

CHAPTER EIGHT

LONG STORY SHORT, I didn't find them a goat. No ruminant deserved that fate. On the other hand, I did jump back on to the constable's motorcycle and demand he gun it before my eyeball twitched itself out of my head. I'd never be able to look at Jimmy again. Good thing he stood way below my eye level.

Over the next hour or so we worked our way through the of Yiayia's old friends and body thieves. Not one of them was home. We checked the local coffee shops. Nothing.

"They could be at church," Pappas said. "Old people love church."

Elderly Greeks did love church. Not just because they were trying to curry favor with God in the twilight of their lives, but also because church was one of the best gossip hubs. And the best of the best on Merope was Ayios Konstantinos—Saint Constantine.

Postcards from Merope frequently feature the island's largest, fanciest church. Like most Greek churches it suffered from excess. King Midas dragged himself to Ayios

Konstantinos to projectile vomit gold on the walls, the domed ceiling, the icons' frames. At the front of the church, Jesus hung from his crucifix, eyes in a perpetual roll, like, "Holy cow, did these clowns learn nothing from Baba's books?"

"All of them?" We were talking about a dozen of Yiayia's closest friends. What were odds they had gone to convene with God at the same time?

"Maybe they've gone to pray for forgiveness. The Bible says people should not steal. They are all old. They could drop dead at any time, so they are probably making peace with God just in case."

He had a point. Unfortunately his phone rang and he suddenly had somewhere else to be. Which meant the person stuck checking out the church was about to be me.

Wasn't all bad news, though. Constable Pappas cheerfully dropped me off at the church so I didn't have to walk. What a prince.

I sighed at the sight of Ayios Konstantinos. There was no denying the hulking structure was photogenic with its brilliant white walls and its blue dome. From the outside it evoked feelings of peace and serenity … in other people. Not me. Trips to this particular church made me feel grubby, like I'd been licking a tourist on their way home from Mykonos.

The reason I felt icky was inside, pacing up and down the church's marble floors as she hurled insults into her phone. Kyria Sofia, sister to Father Spiros, Ayios Konstantinos's priest, was supposed to see someone about a donkey, but they backed out of the meeting. She was not a happy woman.

No sign of Yiayia's thieving troupe. One theory down …

The phone vanished into the handbag dangling neatly

over her gloved wrist when Kyria Sofia spotted me vacillating between coming and fleeing. She smoothed her recently retouched blond twist and adjusted her face until the mouth curved into a smile that was only mostly wolf.

"Aliki! How good of you to share your generosity with us again."

This time she didn't waste a moment steering past the icons, toward the ornate collection box with its shiny lock. She waited expectantly while I pulled a ten-euro note from my purse and wiggled it in to the box. Then she turned her smile on me again. A ten-euro smile. Not as big as the twenty.

"Have you come to speak with God or my brother today?"

Why beat around the bush? "Someone dug up Yiayia's coffin and stole it and her body."

"How distasteful." The way she said it, casually with a lightly wrinkled nose, made it sound like she was judging her least favorite pie at a pie contest. Mind you, it was all relative. Kyria Sofia owns the largest collection of bestiality porn in the northern hemisphere. She hides it behind the respectable facade of a computer folder labeled Sewing. When she's not enjoying her movie nights, she strolls around the island with a stick in her posterior and her nose in the air. She is self-appointed Merope royalty, always first on the scene when VIPs dock at the island.

Also, there's something weird about her relationship with her brother. Maybe they spent too much naked time together as kids.

Despite the folder full of bestiality porn, Kyria Sofia dresses like she's part nun. Today her habit of choice consisted of a navy blue skirt suit with dark tights, sensible heels, and the ever-present ladybug brooch attached to one lapel.

"I won't lie," I lied, "but my family and I are worried sick."

"Of course you are. What a terrible crime. Your grandmother was ..." she went out searching for adjectives "... a person who lived on this island all her life. Do the police have any leads?"

"Not exactly. I was hoping, seeing as how you're a faithful confidante and comfort to so many people, you might have heard something useful."

My thickly layered praise made me want to barf, but it always got the job done. Kyria Sofia loved flattery, and she loved it all over her.

She tapped her chin thoughtfully with a gloved finger. "I do not think I have heard anything ... but maybe my brother ..."

When I swallowed I tasted rancid oil at the back of my throat. Father Spiros reminds me of a lich—an undead creature, a necromancer or king, clinging to this world by magic, long after he should be dead. But that's just me. People all over Merope slobber on the priest's hand every week.

Against my better judgment and animal instincts, I said, "Do you think you could ask him?"

"You can ask him yourself. Come."

I was afraid of that.

Ayios Konstantinos, like most large Greek churches, contained a backroom, where the priest kept his priest gear for services. I'd never been in the back of Ayios Konstantinos, so I was surprised to see it also contained a smallish but opulent office. Lashings of gold. Lots of saints with sad, put-upon expressions, staring down from the walls and windows. Mankind was deeply disappointing to them. It didn't seem helpful to point out that they'd lost Jesus on their watch. At the desk sat Father Spiros. Stock still.

Hands on desk. As though his clockwork guts had wound down. He was a tall, thin man with hooded eyelids and coffee stained teeth. Probably he ate puppies for breakfast.

"Brother?" Kyria Sofia said.

He looked up. He focused. He smiled his puppy-munching smile. "Aliki Callas." He picked up his groovy black priest hat and dropped it onto his head before rising and crossing the small space as though his feet were wheels. "I have heard your name more and more frequently recently."

Decades of living as Greek Orthodox meant the routine came automagically. I asked for his blessing. He gave it and offered me his hand to kiss. His skin felt like paper, as though someone had wrapped him in dead trees before placing him in his chair.

"That is because Aliki is such a generous donor," his sister said. She filled him in about Yiayia's change of address to no address. All the while, Father Spiros nodded.

"It is an abomination, removing the dead from their resting places," he said. "They do that all over Greece these days if you do not have the money to keep them in the ground."

His sister didn't look happy. "Brother …"

"It is true," he said. "If you cannot pay, you cannot stay. But on Merope we do not have that problem. Lots of dirt for lots of bodies. Maybe they took her from one piece of dirt and put her in another piece."

Kyria Sofia glanced at me. Her brother was a spoonful of *tzatziki* short of a gyro and she knew it.

"They were close, the people who took your grand-mother." The priest tented his fingertips. "Close to your Yiayia, yes?"

"Yes. They were her friends."

"Then you do not need worry. Most of the time people do not sexually violate the bodies of their dead friends."

Kyria Sofia made a choking sound. My eye twitched. I shoved my finger into the socket to make it stop. The muscles around my eye kept on seizing.

"Good luck." Father Spiros made the sign of the cross, centimeters away from my nose. "May God watch over your grandmother and never judge her for what her friends are doing to her body."

————

Out in the church, Kyria Aspasia, the church's custodian, slopped water from a metal bucket onto the marble floor. Kyria Aspasia has one eye and a humped back she won in the osteoporosis lottery. Her hump swayed back and forth as she swished the mop.

She grabbed my arm on the way past. "My hump wants to tell you something. I will meet you outside, under the apricot tree." She dumped the mop in the bucket and took off with me struggling to keep up. Nobody has more stamina or speed than old Greek women. It's their super power. Complaints about their legs and feet are a trap.

Kyria Aspasia sprinted across the church courtyard and stopped under what I assumed was an apricot tree. They were trees. Trees aren't really my thing. Without fruit there was no real way for me to tell them apart.

Kyria Sofia stood in the church's open door. She didn't look happy about the church's custodian pulling me aside.

"She just wants me to do a job for her," I called out, not sure if that was true. But I found my morality was happy to flex when necessary. Lying to Kyria Sofia didn't make me feel one bit guilty. "New, hard-to-find cleaning products. Ayios Konstantinos deserves the cleanest church, right?"

The priest's sister wafted away satisfied that this clandestine conversation involved ammonia and bleach.

The church's custodian fixed her one eye on me. The other socket looked like the back end of a cat. "Are you ready to hear what my hump has to say, or are you going to stand there and gossip with the goat-*gameesa* all day?"

I choked. "You know?"

"My hump knows many secrets, including what that woman would like to do with livestock. My hump says Foutoula's friends are trying to bring her back from the dead. That perhaps it was her idea."

Foutoula. Yiayia's name. Toula's name is a hand-me-down from our grandmother.

"Bring Yiayia back from the dead? That's …"

That was what? Impossible? Ghosts were real and yet I was about to quibble about resurrecting the dead?

"What? How? Why?"

She stared at the sky for a long moment, sucking on her empty gums. Eventually she seemed to come to a conclusion. "My hump does not say."

"Does your hump say anything else?"

"Only that it will be a cold, hard winter."

———

A stolen body. A resurrection. The possibility that it was all Yiayia's idea.

My blood pressure did things. Crazy things. A vein in my temple started to throw out beverage ideas. It fancied a bottle of wine. A dry, piney retsina, maybe.

I called Toula.

"Do you think Yiayia is okay with being dead?"

"Is anyone?" Her words slurred. "How would we know anyway?"

"How's that ouzo working out for you?"

"Medicinal. I can hear colors."

The dry, piney retsina went on hold. Toula needed me. Wasn't often I got a shot at playing the big sister.

"Don't go anywhere," I said. "I'm picking up the kids."

School on Merope started at 8:15 and ended at 1:30. It was almost time for Toula to collect Milos and Patra, and she was in no condition to do more than roll off her couch. So I trekked to the Fekkas house to retrieve my bicycle and rode to the low, flat-topped building that served as Merope's elementary school. The structure was c-shaped, the center filled with a large play structure over concrete. No wood chips here, no sir. Here Darwin was king and only the fittest survived. The rest went back inside for a Band-Aid.

I rolled to a stop as the dismissal bell rang. Patra flew out first, her face shining.

"Thea Allie! Guess what?" If she thought my being there was weird it didn't show. "I can do magic. Want to see?" She offered me her pinkie, and because I love her more than life itself, I grabbed it. "Pull," she commanded.

I pulled. She tooted. We dissolved in a puddle of giggles.

Milos was out next, slouching under the weight of his textbook-filled backpack. I took it from him because I cared about his future. Kyria Aspasia and her hump were in my thoughts, and not just for woo-woo reasons. I tucked my tail under and pulled my shoulders back, hoping to ward off future humps.

My nephew glanced around. He knew something was up. "Where is Mama?"

"At home. I begged her to let me pick you guys up."

Patra beamed. "Because you wanted to see my magic trick?"

"That's exactly why."

"Want to see it again?"

"Forever and ever, or until you run out of gas."

"I never run out," she said.

"She's a fart machine," Milos said, almost reverently.

CHAPTER NINE

Toula was on the couch, hugging the ouzo bottle. Her mouth was open. Her eyes were closed. I carefully eased the bottle out and replaced it with a one-eyed pink bunny from Patra's room.

"What's wrong with her?" Milos wanted to know.

Patra raised one of her mother's eyelids. "Is she dead?"

"If she was dead, we'd see her ghost," Milos said.

"She's not dead, she's napping," I told them. "And if she was dead you wouldn't see her ghost for at least forty days."

The front door opened. In came my brother-in-law. He was wearing oil stained coveralls, courtesy of his business, which was fixing cars. Kostas is good and fair in everything he does, including auto repairs. He has red-brown hair, light brown eyes and he has a high tolerance for my sister, which makes him one of life's heroes. He looked at his wife on the couch, his eyebrows high, his expression confused.

"Is that Toula?"

"Possibly a doppelgänger," I said.

"She smells like a *taverna*."

"Someone dug up our grandmother's body and stole it."

"I would drink, too." His gaze wandered toward the kitchen. "Did she cook lunch?"

Priorities. Kostas had them.

"I can make sandwiches," I offered.

"With *tiganites*?"

Thirty minutes later I was feeding my sister's family grilled cheese and mortadella sandwiches, with fries. While everyone ate, Toula slept off the ouzo. After lunch, Kostas pushed out of his chair, thanked me, and left. In winter there was no siesta. Business continued as per usual, for the most part.

The natives were restless and the pull-my-finger routine was starting to wear thin. I couldn't bail yet. Not when Toula and the kids needed me.

"Did someone really steal your *yiayia*'s body?" Milos asked

How much could I say without scarring them for life?

"Do you think they're cannibals?" Patra asked.

Too late. They were already ruined.

"I don't think they're cannibals," I said.

"They might be," she said.

"Yiayia has been dead a long time, and I think cannibals prefer fresh human meat," I said.

"Have you ever met a cannibal?" she asked.

"Not that I know of," I said.

"Then how do you know? Maybe cannibals are like crocodiles and they eat their meat all stinky."

"Can I pull your finger again?" I asked, trying to change the subject.

"If your *yiayia* is dead, then why doesn't she visit us?" Patra asked.

"I don't know, honey. Not everyone comes back as a ghost."

"Why not?"

"Most of the time the dead move on completely and they choose not to come back. Usually if they're here there's a reason. They don't want to leave or can't."

Her forehead wrinkled. That didn't seem to compute. "Why can't they?"

"Reasons. They're watching over loved ones, they have unresolved business, things like that."

"Or, a ghost hunter trapped them," Milos said.

I thought about the jars in Roger Wilson's house and how he'd turned regular ghosts into furious poltergeists by trapping them in salt jars. The ghosts were free now and had all moved on. Only one jar remained, and it was on my coffee table. Its inhabitant was allegedly unique. Call me kooky, but that didn't sound good. The Man in Black had dared me to open it at some point. I wasn't there yet. Maybe I never would be. Especially not after his recent warning to keep it hidden.

"I bet your Yiayia is trapped somewhere," Patra said, "and that's why she doesn't visit us."

My grandmother had loved her great-grandchildren, even more than she loved the vibrating chair she owned for the arthritis she didn't have. If she could have, she would have popped back to visit with them in an instant.

Maybe that was wishful thinking on my part. For all I knew she'd moved on completely, choosing the Afterlife life over regular life. I couldn't blame her. From what little I knew, the Afterlife took care of its citizens. They had fun. They had games. They (eventually) taught the dead how to rattle chains.

Questions passed through my mind. The only answer

to show up was cake. The sudden craving wrestled me out of my seat.

"Wow," I said dramatically. "I wish I knew someone around here that liked cake and sweets."

"We do!" my niece and nephew chimed.

I left a note for Toula—several notes in several places, plus a text message to her phone—and we set off for the Cake Emporium on foot.

Betty had rearranged the front window, again. Winter was starting to creep across the glass, while autumn held on fast to the center and far end. The scarecrow was half snowman, the pumpkins at its feet touched with sparkling sugar frost.

The door flew open. Betty's smile lit up the narrow alley. "Does anyone want hot peppermint chocolate and cookies?"

"It's still November." My protest was pathetic, at best. On the inside I was dissolving in a puddle of drool.

"I can never help myself," she said. "I adore Christmas."

Greek Christmas was starting to merge with the western world's Santa Claus and elf vision of the holiday. Sprigs of basil suspended over a bowl were being replaced with Christmas trees. Every year was more commercial than the last. Business always picked up in December as people on the island began to panic about finding the perfect gift. My Decembers were spent mostly on the internet, stalking auctions and niche retailers.

Milos and Patra fell through the Cake Emporium's door, desperate to reach the promised hot peppermint chocolate. It was already waiting in front of a fireplace that had never been there on previous visits and might never be again. Betty had set out thick cushions for the kids to sit on, along with festive plates of thumbprint cookies and melt-in-the-mouth linzers.

"I knew you were coming, so I took liberties," she said. "How's your sister then, love?"

"She's playing Cleopatra, Queen of Denial."

"It'll be fine. Before you know it your grandma will be back in the ground where she belongs." She made a face. "I don't know if that's true, but I have faith in your ability to find things."

Normally I did, too. But with Yiayia, I wasn't sure where to start. I had a missing body and a bunch of absent senior citizens—two of them dead. Where could the island hide that many people and a coffin and keep it a secret? If there was such a place, there was no way they wouldn't be spotted hauling a dirt-caked casket.

When I asked Betty, she said, "You know this island better than I do, love. All I know is my little piece of it."

I worked through the possibilities. "The rec center? No. Too many eyes and ears. That's the problem with most of Merope. You can't keep things like stolen bodies a secret."

"You might have to step out of your comfort zone. There's help all over this island if you're willing to let more incorporeal beings know you can see them."

My eyebrows took a hike. "Tell ghosts I can see them?"

A handful knew. People like Vasili Moustakas, and the dockworkers and sailors who never strayed from the waterfront. I chose carefully, and only revealed my secret if absolutely necessary. The last thing I needed was every ghost on the island showing up, demanding my time and attention. Ghosts used to be people but they're not people. Unencumbered by things like bodies and consequences, they're walking, talking, comment sections.

"Would that be so bad?" She nudged the cookie plate

closer to me. I sought comfort in a raspberry linzer that dusted the front of my sweater with powdered sugar.

"If ghosts know I can see and hear them, they'll never leave me alone. They'll drive me up the wall."

"Then perhaps you need to choose a select few."

"Any ideas?"

She considered my question while she refilled the children's mugs. "The knowledge keepers. The spirits who, in life, knew things."

Who knew things on Merope? I felt like she meant people with more professional heft than the island's busybodies, who considered their opinions to be on par with facts.

"Librarians," I said.

She clapped her tiny, delicate hands. "Perfect! Librarians know almost everything. If they don't know it, they know how to find it. Seems to me like you'd have a lot in common, no?"

———

Merope's library is housed in a two-story building the color of pale sand, with golden yellow shutters and a matching door. The little balconies are filled with potted plants. It looks like someone's home. The library isn't massive, but it's better than adequate. Its catalog includes an oddball variety of foreign language books—mostly English. Tourists leave books behind en masse when the packing starts and they're forced to choose between souvenirs and reading material they swore they'd read but never did. Those orphaned books—most commonly beach reads—wind up in Merope's library. Toula and I consume them like chips.

The library employs one librarian, Popi Papadopoulou.

She runs the library, acquires new books when she can, and holds story times for preschoolers, twice a week. She does voices. Little kids love voices. Popi is one of those people whose face smiles even when she's not smiling. She's blond, soft, and she knows everything there is to know about books.

And hopefully the island.

Betty intended for me to consult with the ghosts of librarians past. The idea didn't thrill me. So I decided to start with the present's librarian. She knew things. Maybe she knew things I needed to know.

Popi lit up as Patra and Milos burst in ahead of me. Patra threw herself into Popi's arms. My niece didn't ask the librarian to pull her finger, I noticed. Milos played it cool for two seconds before succumbing to the warm hug.

I got it. I kind of wanted to hug Popi, too. She was cookies and milk in human form.

"I come bearing questions," I said. "Research questions, specific to Merope."

"Someone stole my great-grandma's body and they're probably cannibals," Patra said helpfully.

I smiled. What else could I do?

We weren't alone in the library. A smattering of Merope's citizens perused the shelves for reading material. There were others, too. Ghosts of librarians past. The former librarians prowled the stacks, transparent fingers running along the spines. In death they were still picky about what went where. Librarians never quit libraries. I recognized one as Popi's predecessor. She'd died on the job after a philosophy shelf collapsed on her head.

"Cannibals!" Popi pretend to be horrified in a dramatic way that kids eat up. "That's crazy! I love cannibals!" She crouched down in front of them. "If I was a cannibal, do you know what I'd eat?"

"People?" Milos said.

"Books!"

That didn't make a lick of sense, seeing as how cannibals eat people. That's why they're called cannibals. But my niece and nephew didn't care. All they knew was that they adored Popi.

She ushered Patra and Milos to the children's area and came back to me. "Cannibals? Really?"

"Not cannibals—not that I know of, anyway. Although you never really know about people. But the stolen grandmother part is true."

"And so you're looking for what, exactly?"

"My grandmother's friends took her. A dozen or so of them. They've vanished. The island isn't that big. There's a limit to where they could be hiding out with a coffin."

"Merope's gossip network?"

"Silent. Nobody saw anything or it would be everywhere."

"True. They didn't get a transport off the island?"

I tilted my chin up then down, declaring a Greek *no*. That many old folks and a coffin, someone would have seen them board a boat.

"The old church?"

The church at Merope's crest, Ayia Paraskevi—Saint Friday— was reduced to rubble during an earthquake decades ago. These days nobody went there to pray unless it was to pray they wouldn't be caught cooking *sisa*—Greek meth.

"Not enough cover. I don't suppose any of the responsible parties have taken out any interesting books lately?"

Behind her, the dead librarians were beginning to take notice of our conversation. They moved closer, alert and listening and exchanging glances. Did they know something Popi didn't? I tried not to make eye contact. Not yet. Not unless it was a last resort.

"I can check for you, no problem."

I gave her the list of Yiayia's friends, the faces I'd witnessed stealing her remains. Popi's fingers flew over the keyboard.

"This is interesting," she said. "What I can tell you is that they developed a sudden interest in the occult a few weeks ago. They've all been checking out books dealing with ghosts, necromancy, and Harry Potter. No, wait, that's Kyrios Psaris, and it's the twenty-third time he's checked out the whole series. But they're all really into urban fantasy and paranormal romance—and have been for a long time."

Surprise buttered my face. I couldn't see it but I could feel it: high eyebrows, slightly open mouth, dumb expression. "Really?"

"You'd be amazed what people read. I can't keep Young Adult books on the shelves. Old women love them. Old men, too."

So Yiayia's old posse had a newfound interested in the occult, resurrecting the dead, urban fantasy, and they'd made some kind of promise to bring her back. A promise to whom? Yiayia? I needed to know these things, and I needed to get my grandmother back in the ground where she belonged. As much as I loved her, her time was up.

Wasn't it?

"I don't suppose there's a rumored super secret mystical place on Merope that a group of confused elderly people with a weird interest in the paranormal might gravitate towards?"

"Merope is old, and you'd think it would be riddled with religious ruins, but everything we have is unremarkable, except for its age. Old village foundations, that sort of thing. Nothing mystical, as far as I know."

She was right and I knew it. Merope's allure was in its beaches and sunshine and stereotypical Greek charm. People looking for ancient culture gravitated toward places that radiated history, like Delphi, and Athens, and Delos with its stone lions.

The long gone librarians gathered around the circulation desk, tutting. I avoided eye contact. They knew something—more than the current librarian knew. If only there was some way to squeeze them for information without giving up the jig. Something told me letting librarians know I could see and hear them would backfire on me spectacularly. These dead women were potential information mega conduits.

"Thanks anyway," I said. "Milos, Patra. Time to go."

Popi wasn't done with me. "I have a wishlist."

I held out my hand. She smiled her sweet, temperate smile. Out came a piece of paper with a list of titles and authors. Way out of print books. Old. Some of them older than others.

I thanked Popi for her time, promised to locate the books on her wish list, and gathered up my niece and nephew, who refused to leave without a dozen books apiece. Patra's pile was all about poop and butts.

"It's for my magic," she told me.

I couldn't argue with that. The girl had ambition.

CHAPTER TEN

TOULA WAS WAKING up to the knowledge that ouzo wasn't her best friend after all.

"What happened?" Her makeup said she'd caught a fist with her eyes. Her hair said she'd fallen into a pedestal fan. Saliva had formed a map of Africa on her cheek and dried to white flakes.

"Ouzo," I said. "Ouzo happened. It does that."

"Not to me," Toula said.

"There's a first time for everything."

"And a last," she muttered on her way to the bathroom. I heard sounds of toothbrushing. Before long, Toula reappeared with her makeup and hair where they belonged. "Did they find Yiayia?"

"Not yet."

She shuddered. Her gaze slid to the empty ouzo bottle. I snatched it up and tucked it under my arm.

"They'll find her," I said.

"Is Leo working on it?"

"Constable Pappas."

"Isn't he twelve?"

"I think he's at least fourteen," I said about the baby-faced cop. "Leo's busy with other cases."

Toula waited for an explanation. I didn't give her one. If she couldn't handle grave robbery, then stabbings on spirit boards would have her prowling the island, hunting for more ouzo.

I waved the bottle at her. "I'll recycle this for you."

I rode home and Googled the history of Merope. The dead librarians knew things, which meant the knowledge was out there, just not in Popi's head. Maybe the internet knew. I focused on fringe groups and conspiracy theorists. It's always risky dealing with people with a tenuous grasp on reality. But sometimes they know the best, truest stuff. Man did walk on the moon. Earth is in fact round and not pancake flat.

"*Psst.*"

I stuck a finger in my ear, wiggled. Had somebody *psst* at me or was it a bug in my ear?

Please don't be a bug, I thought. I can handle *pssting*, but if I had a bug in my ear I'd never sleep again.

"*Psst.*"

No bug. Definitely someone *pssting* at me.

I swiveled around. Konstantinos Grivas was hunkered down behind my couch, transparent and floating a centimeter above the floor.

"Did you find my killer?" he asked me.

"Was I supposed to? Wait—you know about that?"

"I overheard the policeman telling you."

"Eavesdropping is rude."

"So is murder."

He had a point.

"No, I haven't found your murderer, and I don't intend to. That's police business. The police get grumpy when you interfere in their investigations."

That didn't seem to faze the ghost. He looked furtively left and right. "If you see Yiorgos Dakis, do not tell him I was here."

"Why not?"

"He will be angry."

"So? Let him be angry. He's dead, and so are you. Now shoo. I have work to do."

"I have a list of suspects."

"Murder suspects?"

"No—people who stole my *kolos*. Of course murder suspects."

I waited. No list appeared. "Where's the list?"

He tapped his transparent temple. "In here."

"How is that going to help the police?"

"The police?" He had the audacity to look shocked, as if the police weren't the right people for the job.

"Detective Samaras is already working on your case. He wouldn't be happy if I interfered. So spit out the names, I'll write them down, and then I'll give them to the detective.

"If you are not going to work on this then I will not give you the names."

"Fine," I said. "But before you go could you tell me why you and your friends stole my grandmother?"

"Uh, do I have to?"

"Yes."

"What will happen if I do not tell you?"

"Something bad."

He waited.

"Something very bad," I went on.

A hand appeared out of thin air, latched on to his arm, and yanked him out of my apartment. I recognized it as Yiorgos Dakis' hairy appendage.

"Rude," I said to no one in particular.

I called Leo. "Any luck with the murder?"

"No. Any luck finding your grandmother's body?"

"No. But your murder victim was here with a suspect list. Of course he didn't get a chance to give it to me."

"We're looking at the wife," he said, "although we're not actually looking at the wife because she's disappeared."

"Her and everyone involved with Yiayia's theft."

"Pappas said they had all vanished. Where do you think they are?"

"I'm working on a theory."

"What is it?"

"I'm working on that, too."

"So you've got nothing?" He sounded amused.

"I've got a lead," I said, wincing.

What I had were dead librarians who may or may not know a thing. And I didn't technically have them yet because I hadn't mustered up the gumption to let them I know I could see them.

"Have you eaten?" he asked.

"Not yet."

Someone knocked on my door.

"Hold on," I said into the phone. I opened the door. Leo was standing there with a bag of food. Gyros and fries, by the smell of it.

"I figured," he said.

"I'm not saying I love you, but right now I definitely could."

He leaned down and kissed me lightly. My hormones flipped out. "I should bring you food more often."

"You really should."

Normally we ate at the table, but this time Leo unpacked the bags on the coffee table. I rustled up plates, salt, napkins, water. We sat on the couch side by side and ate in silence for the next five minutes.

Giggles broke out behind us.

I groaned into the gyro. We had company.

Succubi.

Contrary to belief, the demon women don't suck blood and party with Dracula. They collect men the way some people collect Pokemons. The men live normal lives, without the slightest suspicion they're being observed … and occasionally swapped for a different man in another succubus's collection. Whatever frequency I was wired into that allowed me to see ghosts also tapped into the succubus channel. At first Bleeder and Choker—my pet names for them, based on our initial meeting—tried to send me fleeing by faking murder-by-Leo while we were on our first fancy date. It almost worked. I ditched Leo to crawl out the restaurant's bathroom window. Then I got smart and called their bluff.

For some inexplicable reason, Leo's succubi always chose mealtimes to show up. Thankfully they'd dropped the homicide angle and presented as regular women instead of murder victims now. The succubi are tall, thin, flawless. Perfect outer skins for the puke-worthy demons hiding underneath. These two spoil the whole effect by dressing like they're on their way to their favorite street corner in a dodgy neighborhood.

"Why do you always dress like sex workers?" I asked them. "Not that there's anything wrong with that particular line of work, provided everyone is consenting and no one is getting exploited. But you have an entire world of fashion to choose from."

"Worlds," one of them said.

I rolled my eyes. "Worlds then."

Leo made a weird, strangling noise into his gyro, but he didn't stop eating or turn around. Was he getting accustomed to the weirdness or merely resigned?

The succubus shrugged off my sarcasm. "We can change, if you like."

In an instant, Bleeder was Marie Antoinette, with a birdcage in her powdered wig, a small winged llama hunched on the perch inside.

"Is that a llama?"

"It might be," she said. "What's a llama?"

On our first meeting she was the one bleeding on my dinner. Her pal choked as she expired from strangulation. It was all wildly theatrical at the time.

"Do you two have names? Because in my head you're just acts of violence."

"Names," Bleeder said. "We have names." She made a sound like she was gargling drain cleaner. "Now you try saying it."

My food was suddenly less appealing. "Never mind."

"You can give us names if it makes you feel better … or if it makes you feel worse. We do not care. We are above such things."

"We are just here for him, anyway," her friend said.

"True story," Bleeder said.

"But I always liked the name Jezebel," Choker told me.

Bleeder nodded like she knew. "Now there was a woman who stood up for what she believed in."

"Jezebel was real?" I tried munching on a fry. No flavor left. It would take an act of feta and eggs to fix these potatoes. "Never mind. I don't care. I'll call you whatever you want me to call you, Jezebel. It was better than what I was calling you in my head."

"What about me?" the other one said. "Don't I get a name, too?"

"You didn't want one a minute ago," Jezebel said.

She pouted prettily. "Well, things change. Now I want one. A woman can change her mind. It's her prerogative."

"That's very human of you," I said.

She snarled. For a moment the woman skin fell away and I caught a glimpse of demon. It wasn't pretty under there, let me tell you. A mixture of puke and crap and fangs and boils. Some things the human eye isn't supposed to see.

"Tiffany it is then," I said, suddenly nauseated. "You seem like a sweet, perky Tiffany."

"Tiffany," Leo muttered. "Jezebel. Ungh." He crammed fries into his mouth and resumed chewing.

"Since you two crashed dinner," I said, "do you think you could be useful?"

"We don't do dishes," Jezabel said. "Just so we are clear."

I rooted around for a napkin. "Information."

"We don't do information," Jezebel said.

"Unless we can wreck havoc and cause confusion," Tiffany told me.

"Then we do information," Jezebel agreed.

I located the napkin, wiped my fingers, dropped it next to the fries I'd maybe never eat. "Someone—a bunch of someone's dug up my grandmother's coffin and stole it and her."

Jezebel made gagging sounds. "Necromancers. Gross. I kept one in my collection once for a whole year. He always smelled like dirt. I wound up swapping him for an accountant because I could not handle the stink. He was pretty, though. Sometimes I miss his face, even though he no longer has one."

Leo didn't know how lucky he was, hearing only my side of the conversation. What was going through his head?

I decided to be sneaky. "You two know a lot, huh?"

"We know things," Jezebel said.

"I bet you know all about this island."

"We know where all the cute men are," she said.

"And the cute shoes," Tiffany added.

"If you were going to hide something here, where would you hide it?"

"A game!" Tiffany clapped. "I love games."

"I hate games," Jezebel said. "Unless someone is screaming or crying. Then I love games. This doesn't sound like that kind of game."

"There's probably screaming and crying," I said. Or there would be when I got my hands on Yiayia's sticky-fingered friends. "If you were going to hide something on this island, like, say, a coffin and a dozen senior citizens, where would you hide them?"

"I don't like old people," Jezebel said. "Especially old men. They smell funny and they wear big underpants."

"These old people, are they dead?" Tiffany wanted to know.

"Alive," I said.

"In the cave," Tiffany said.

"Merope doesn't have caves. It's a big chunk of rock."

"Ha!" She peered down her nose at me. "That's what you think."

"That's what everyone thinks." Except that wasn't true, was it? The dead librarians knew things even the current librarian didn't know. "How is a cave a secret? Seems like someone would know."

"It's there," Tiffany said. "Like a cavity in a tooth."

"Where?"

"Boring," Jezebel said. "All this conversation is making me wish I had someone to torture. I don't suppose you two could hurry up and have sex. We like watching sex."

"Nobody is having sex!" I said.

Leo lowered the gyro. He gave me a slow, lazy grin. "Now you tell me."

My face went up in flames. "Have you ever heard anything about a cave?"

He blinked, confused. "Are we still talking about sex?"

"No. A real cave."

"On Merope? No. It's solid rock."

My brain kicked in to overthinking mode. I scoffed down a couple of the fries I'd sworn I was done eating.

As soon as Popi the librarian went home and the sun went down, I was going back to the library.

CHAPTER ELEVEN

Is it breaking and entering if you're only entering and not breaking? I worked through the argument in my head as I rode to the library. Look at me, pretending to be a Greek philosopher.

The library wasn't locked. It never is. There's no return slot. Instead, if you want to return a book after hours, you can waltz right in and leave it on the counter.

I slipped inside and closed the door behind me.

In the dark, the library was a different creature. Most things are when you remove the spotlight. Instead of welcoming, with the strange, calm current mass quantities of books tend to emit, tonight the library seemed to vibrate with an inaudible warning. There was knowledge here, but to access it you better have your library card ready, or else. And the book gods help you if you didn't return your reading material on time.

Ghost librarians roamed between the stacks, judgmental and stern, even in death. Popi was a new, bright flavor of librarian. These women were old school. Make noise at your peril, and never enter the building with food or liquids.

I cleared my throat. Quietly. Like meerkats, their heads rose and swiveled in my direction.

"I'm looking for information," I said in a low, respectful voice. I wanted their help, not their ire. I dangled the bait. "Could you please help me?"

They couldn't resist.

Kyria Chrysanthi floated forward. In death the library's previous librarian still dressed for the job she'd committed to in life. Severe gray pencil skirt that terminated mid calf. High-buttoned blouse. Sweater vest. Her hair was caught up in the same strict bun she wore every day of her life, without a single escapee strand.

"Come back when the library is open," one of the other librarians said. They cackled. Kyria Chrysanthi snapped her judgmental gaze to them. The cackling quit.

"Aliki Callas," she said. "I remember you. No late books. No books harmed while they were in your care. I will help you."

Excited chatter broke out.

"Wait—she can see us?"

"She can see us!"

"Shh!" Kyria Chrysanthi pointed to the sign on the wall, the one with all the library rules. "Being dead is no excuse for being loud."

"I can see you," I admitted, "and I need your help. Earlier when I was here, you acted as if you knew something about my grandmother's stolen body."

Kyria Chrysanthi made a face. "The new librarian is young and inexperienced. She is so busy with new programs at the library, programs that have nothing to do with books, that she has forgotten what she is."

"A librarian?" I said.

"A librarian. Librarians know things, and what they do not know they know how to find. They keep order. They help when it is required. And to do so they must also be in constant pursuit of new knowledge … and old."

"Am I correct in assuming you possess that old knowledge?"

"Of course! Merope's librarians have always kept a diary of sorts. A logbook. In it we record all the island's secrets as we uncover them, in hopes that they might one day be useful to someone. It passes from librarian to librarian. The new librarian has the diary, but she is so busy that she has barely skimmed the pages. She has mistaken it for a sentimental trinket, not an object of intellectual value."

"Today might be that day," I said.

Her face hardened. "Unfortunately the logbook has gone missing."

"Stolen," one of the other librarians said in a low voice. "Stolen from right under our noses."

"People have always stolen knowledge from libraries," Kyria Chrysanthi said. "They seek to keep the information out of the minds of others, or they wish to hoard it for themselves. They know nothing of true knowledge. The answers are all out there if you know where and how to look."

"Knowing the Dewey Decimal Classification System helps," a librarian from the 1970s said.

"Or your alphabet," said another, from an earlier time period I recognized as post-World War II.

"We would be grateful if you found the library's logbook," Kyria Chrysanthi said.

"You want to hire me?"

"We cannot pay you with anything so crude as money, but we can compensate you in other ways. We are Merope's knowledge base, after all."

Money wasn't crude. Money paid the bills. The electric company refused to accept information in exchange for electricity, unless that information was my bank account details. But being able to dip into a new well of information would come in handy in my line of work.

"Deal," I said. "But tonight I have an immediate problem. I need to find my grandmother's body and the people who took her. Where could they be? Someone—well, something—mentioned caves on Merope. I didn't know there was such a thing."

"There are no caves on Merope," she said. "But there is a cavern under the island. God did not make it though. It was carved by ancient man."

"Women, actually," another librarian said.

"Man, woman, same thing," another said.

"No—not the same thing at all," Kyria Chrysanthi said. "There you go trying to erase women's accomplishments. Women made the cavern for women's business."

"Women's business?" I asked.

"Listen to her," a librarian from the turn of last century said, disgusted. "She knows nothing about her own kind. What do women do?"

"Anything they want?" I said. "Girl power?"

"No—what do they do? Your answer is an answer for t-shirts and those stickers people put on the backs of their cars. What do women *do*?"

I waited.

And waited some more.

Nobody ponied up an answer.

"Can I call a friend or Google it?" I asked.

One of the librarians threw her hands in the air, waving them ala Kermit the Frog. "They give life!"

The computer that was my brain wasn't computing.

"Are you saying they excavated the island so they could give birth?"

One of the long-dead librarians beckoned. "Come."

I followed her between the stacks. She led me through the classics. Newer classics. Greek classics were older than most and had their own shelves deeper in the library. We stopped in front of a row of leather-bound books. She pointed. The tip of her finger vanished to the first knuckle, through Mary Shelley's *Frankenstein*.

"They created the cavern to bring back the dead," she told me. "If your grandmother is anywhere, she is there."

"And she is probably no longer dead," another librarian said.

Living people didn't bother me. Ghosts didn't bother me … beyond their magnified personality flaws. But the undead? The idea of zombie Yiayia stumbling around, possibly demanding a light snack of my brains made my blood run cold.

We returned to the circulation desk.

"Where is this cavern?" I asked.

"I can show you." Kyria Chrysanthi led me over to the map of Merope that hung on the library wall. It was bare as far as maps went. We had one main village and no forests, lakes, or any other serious landmarks that usually dictate points of interest on a map. So the mapmaker had added things like churches, long-standing farms, and the spot where an ancient fisherman had allegedly caught a shark that granted him wishes. There was some talk that the shark was actually Zeus in disguise, not for any reason other than talking animals usually turned out to be Zeus.

She jabbed a finger at the map.

The cavern was under a goat farm. Yikes.

The library's door handle rattled. The librarians faded back into their beloved stacks. Heart pounding, I crouched down behind the desk and held my breath as the door creaked open. There wasn't time to act normally, like I was returning books.

Footsteps entered. Not boots. These clicked as they struck the floor. The reader was wearing high heels. Probably a woman. Or a cautious man who only wore heels after dark. Merope was home to a dozen or so cross-dressers, all with superior-to-mine makeup skills.

The reader carefully laid his or her books on the counter. A stack of them by the sounds of it. I held my breath and tried to be invisible.

Lydia's face appeared over the top of the circulation desk. She looked amused. "Lose something?"

My breath released in a rush. Relief washed over me.

"I dropped a book," I said.

"Don't tell the librarian."

"That you were here?"

"That you dropped a book."

I blew out a sigh and slowly stood. My gaze cut to Lydia's freshly returned books. Romance novels. Who'd have guessed that? Not me. Lydia's hobbies involved sex, floggings, and incomprehensible German heavy metal. Romance didn't fit. I figured her for a horror junkie.

When it came to people, you just never knew what they were hiding under their wrapping paper.

Lydia caught me staring. "I read them for the romance."

"I figured you read them for the sex."

"I have sex for the sex."

That made sense. I changed the subject before things got weird.

"My grandmother's friends stole her body and I think they're trying to reanimate her, Frankenstein-style, in a secret underground cavern. I was here trying to find the location of the cavern."

And just like that I'd made things weirder.

Lydia didn't so much as blink. "Did you find it?"

"Finding stuff is my thing."

"Where is it?"

"Under a goat farm."

"What are you waiting for?"

"For you to leave."

"Not a chance," she said. "This is the most interesting thing that's happened on Merope since I've been here. Goats, stolen grandmothers, secret caverns, the possibility a bunch of old people will turn your grandmother into a zombie."

Nobody in this world wanted zombie Yiayia. She'd be lurching around the island, devouring penis instead of brains.

"Virgin Mary. I really hope I don't have to put a stake in zombie Yiayia."

"Relax," she said with a too-cheerful smile. "Stakes are for vampires. To kill a zombie you need to cut of its head. Let's go."

We'd freeze to death out there. Not to mention it was private property. Sneaking around in the dark was a good way to wind up on the wrong end of a wooden spoon or a flying slipper.

That's what I told Lydia, anyway.

"Come on. Live a little," she said.

"I'm more worried about dying a lot."

"It's just goats. What could they possibly do?"

I raised an eyebrow at her.

CHAPTER TWELVE

"I TAKE IT BACK," Lydia said. "This was a terrible idea, and now we're going to die by goat."

We were surrounded by goats. Dozens of horned and hungry beasts rooted through our pockets, hunting for snacks or anything that could pass as a snack. One goat inhaled a tissue I'd used twice and forgotten to toss out.

"I did warn you," I said.

"What do we do?"

"Do you have any real snacks?"

Goats trampled over us. They weren't big on personal space.

"I don't snack. Have you seen my clothes?"

"Barely."

"Exactly."

"Then we're definitely going to die by goat," I said. "And we haven't even found the entrance to the cavern yet." Some pervert of a billy goat chomped down on my coat's zipper and tugged, almost yanking me off my feet. I seized his horns, put serious effort in to shoving him away. "Hey, that's my coat! I need it so I don't freeze!"

The goats didn't care. They kept on coming. Our deaths would eventually be imminent, once they ran out of clothing to consume.

Crumbs fell out of the sky.

The goats broke off their relentless snuffling to chase gritty bits of baked goods. I helped Lydia up off the ground.

She aimed her phone at my face. I winced. "There's a hoof print on your forehead," she pointed out.

"I'm trying a new look."

More crumbs scattered across the area. Someone had perfect timing—and snacks. After locating my flashlight, I panned it in the direction of the crumbs.

"Who's there?"

I lowered the beam of light. Lowered it again. Until it hit hair.

"Fuck the Virgin Mary with a horn, are you trying to blind me?" Jimmy Kontos said. He was holding a huge bag of mini chocolate cakes. "I'm trying to save you, and this is the thanks I get."

"What are you doing out here?" I hissed.

He looked shifty. "Nothing."

"Were you following us?"

"Maybe. Or maybe I was scouting new locations for tomorrow's scenes. Does it matter? I saved you. What are you doing here?"

Lydia picked up a lump of crumbs, sniffed. "Nice," she said. "Did you make them yourself?"

In the pale light, the praise turned Jimmy pink. "Bought them from a friend. My cousin's a policeman. It's not like I can bake them in his place."

"Leo won't let you bake in his apartment?" I asked. That didn't sound like Leo. Leo loved cake.

Lydia raised an eyebrow at me. She was good at it, like

her grandmother before her. The coin circled the well and plopped right in. Oh. O-o-o-o-h. These weren't just any baked goods. They were sweets with a plus-one special guest star ingredient.

"Is that safe for goats?" I asked.

"They'll eat barbed wire and you're asking if a little cannabis will hurt them?" Jimmy said. "They're goats! They almost trampled you to death!"

To be fair, the goats seemed fine.

Plop.

A goat fell over on its side. It lay there, legs stuck straight out, stiff and unmoving.

To be fair, most of the goats seemed fine.

Plop, plop, plop.

The goats began to drop like flies. Some of the goats seemed fine, although that number was rapidly dwindling. The downed goats started to snore.

Jimmy stared with wonder at the half-full bag of cannabis-loaded cakes in his hand.

"Don't," I said. "You saw what it did to the goats."

He crammed a handful into his mouth and chewed as fast as he could. "You're not my mother." Crumbs sprayed out. "You can't tell me what to do."

"Wow. You're making a great impression." My gaze flicked to Lydia, who was crouched down several meters away, checking the goats for life signs.

"I can't help myself," he said, lowering his voice. "I get crazy when I'm nervous."

"Why? She's just a girl—almost literally."

"She's a goddess," he said through the crumbs.

"You'd better get out of here before your feel-good sweets hit."

"Leave? Which one of us is getting high? I'm staying right here. You two obviously need protecting."

I opened my mouth to protest, but damned if the little squirt wasn't right. Goats had almost taken us down, and the only thing that had saved us was a little guy with a jumbo bag of edibles. Who knew what we'd encounter if we managed to find the cavern?

"Fine. At the very least you can help us look."

"What are we looking for?"

"An underground cavern."

"I can do that," he said. "I'm good at scouting for places low to the ground, seeing as how I'm about as tall as a Great Dane."

"Now you're just exaggerating," I told him.

Lydia rejoined us. "The goats are fine," she said. "Just high."

"Is it just me or did it work a little fast?"

She shrugged. "Maybe goat metabolisms process weed faster."

I looked at Jimmy, who suddenly flopped down on the ground and leopard-crawled toward a gnarly olive tree with an outhouse sheltered under its branches.

"I think their metabolisms are fine. That weed on the other hand …"

"What is he doing?" Lydia asked.

"Pretending to be a Great Dane, I think."

"He's funny."

"You have no idea."

Jimmy crept along the ground at the speed of molasses, all the way up to the outhouse. "It's here," he announced.

That seemed unlikely. "In the outhouse?"

"Underneath."

"It's an outhouse."

"Is it?"

He reached up for the handle and missed. He tried again. Missed.

"It keeps moving." He cackled. "Also, it's made of soup."

My stomach growled. "What kind of soup?"

He thought about it for a moment. "*Avgolemono*." Egg and lemon.

"With or without chicken?"

"With meatballs," he said.

Boy, that sounded good. I really wanted to be at home with soup and meatballs instead of standing outside an outhouse, hunting for my grandmother's stolen remains. But no, here I was. This was my reality.

What was Leo doing? Hopefully something warmer than this, with fewer goats.

"That's just an outhouse," Lydia pointed out.

The more I thought about it, the less sure I was. Maybe the little guy was on to something. For the most part this parcel of land was featureless. We'd searched for trap doors and suspicious looking boulders. But there was nothing except dirt, grass too stubborn to die, twisted trees, and goats. "Who puts an outhouse in the middle of nowhere?"

"A goatherd with bladder issues?" Lydia said.

Was she kidding? "Have you met men? They pee anywhere. No official toilet required."

"We *kaka* anywhere, too," Jimmy said helpfully.

I grabbed Jimmy by the ankles and pulled him out of the way. He giggled and rolled over. His eyes were down to a thin sliver of iris. Whatever was in the baked goods it packed a punch.

"Do it again," he said.

I dragged him a little further.

"Again."

I stepped over him to yank open the outhouse door.

Surprise, surprise. No toilet, no bucket, no stack of newspapers or magazines. Instead, there was a set of double doors in the floor where the toilet was supposed to be, not unlike doors to a basement shelter in America's Tornado Alley. They were metal, and the padlock lay slack beside them.

Fear wibble-wobbled my knees. Entering those doors was about as appealing as going for a second round of goat mauling. But the seniors couldn't be allowed to tick reanimating Yiayia off their bucket lists. If they wanted to play zombie, let them find another candidate. Preferably one not related to me.

"Cover me," I said. "I'm going in. And by cover me I mean call the police if you hear me crying, screaming, or if I'm otherwise unable to be sarcastic."

"No sarcasm, got it," Lydia said. She was right behind me.

"Stay and look after the little guy," I told her.

"I'm really bad at doing what other people tell me to do," she said.

"You're your grandmother's granddaughter," I said.

"Thank you."

With my gut clenched and my heart flipping out, I opened the doors. Hot air rushed out. Followed by a blast of Arctic wind. Invisible feet thundered toward us. The flashlight cast jagged light on stone steps. My hand didn't get the memo about staying steady in the face of imminent danger.

"Something's coming," I said. "Quite a few of them."

Lydia's voice was close behind me. "I don't hear anything."

Ghosts. If she couldn't hear them then they were dead. They were coming right for us, and they were … bickering?

"People today, they cannot even perform a proper resurrection," a woman was saying. "*Po-po* … my feet hurt.

I am dead and my feet still hurt. Why me? What did I do to deserve this?"

"That is Kalliope and Yianni's daughter, Eugenia. She was always useless. She could not resurrect a living chicken. Remember when she was a child? Dead behind the ears then, too."

"And what about the Papagiannis boy? *Po-po* … What a malakas. I told his mother not to have any more children, to put it in her mouth instead, but did she listen?"

"I am thinking no, she did not listen."

"She told me that is why a *poutsa* has hair around it, to keep you from putting it in your mouth."

My eye twitched.

"How long have we been down there?" a voice asked.

"Since we died during the last resurrection that went wrong."

"But how long was that?"

"Too long. My feet … my feet … Why did they build so many steps?"

"I cannot believe that old witch slammed the door so we could not leave earlier."

"The living cannot see us, you know that."

"Even if she could see us, that one would not have released us. Her soul is black and mean. Her parents would be ashamed."

Someone spat.

The chorus of complaints continued up the steps until the see-through jumble of ghosts appeared, hobbling and limping towards the exit.

"And look, here are some more *vlakes* waiting to go down," one of the ghosts said. "This must be the backup crew. Maybe they can get the job done."

Under the circumstances, I wasn't sure I objected to being called stupid.

"Who are they trying to resurrect this time anyway?"

"Foutoula Callas."

"*Po-po*." A dead woman crossed herself. "As if they do not have enough problems."

My eyelid fluttered again. Otherwise, I didn't react. The last thing I needed was more attention than the curious glances I was getting.

"She saw me!" one of the ghosts said. He stopped to wave a transparent hand in front of my face.

"People cannot see us," the dead woman who'd besmirched Yiayia's appalling reputation said. "I just told you that."

"Some can, and I am telling you this one can."

Virgin Mary. This I needed like an extra hole in my head.

"Can you still hear the weird noise?" Lydia asked.

I shook my head. "Must have been nothing."

"She can hear us!" the ghost said. "I knew it. Wait—I am going to try something."

The ghost planted himself on the top step, right in the middle, and grabbed his crotch. To get down those stairs I was going to have to walk through him. I hated walking through ghosts. Their unearthly bodies were cold and clammy. Plus it struck me as bad manners to walk through a ghost like they weren't there. They might not be human anymore but they were still people-shaped things.

No way could I balk now. I had to suck it up and walk through the dead man. It was that or attract the attention of all these ghosts. They'd be all up in my face with a wish list of to-dos before I could flinch.

"Well," I said cheerfully. "I'm going down."

Jimmy sat bolt upright. "I just saw my *papou's* balls. He almost tea-bagged my face." He shuddered. He fell backwards, landing with a dull *thud*.

"Drugs. Not even once," I said to no one in particular. I took a step. The crotch-grabbing ghost belched. Was that even possible? The science wasn't there. A woman's transparent hand came out of nowhere and slapped him upside the head.

"Manners," she said.

"Your mother's *mouni*," he said. That earned him another slap.

I pulled on my metaphorical big girl panties and stepped through the dead man. He made a disappointed sound.

"I would have sworn she could see us."

Mentally, I gave myself a high-five. Now to tackle the rest of the steps. I aimed the flashlight's beam at them. There seemed to be no bottom. Down and down they went, in a tight spiral. The air grew thicker, the dark turned to something deeper and deadlier than black. Black with alligators or raw chicken, maybe.

Footsteps followed me down. I had company whether I wanted it or not. And to be honest, I kind of did. It's better to be scared with acquaintances than alone. Lydia didn't speak much, and Jimmy sang songs to himself. Mostly songs about his penis and sexual prowess. His self-advertising campaign was in full swing.

When all hope was lost, and I thought walking down steps was my life now, the darkness thinned out and turned to orange, flickering light.

"Is this hell?" Lydia asked behind me.

"We're Greek Orthodox. We don't believe in physical hell."

"That doesn't mean it's not real and here on Merope."

"Technically *in* Merope."

Voices wafted toward us. More bickering. But these

were real people. I could tell by the way Lydia grabbed my arm and nodded toward the source of the noise.

"Do all the bones go in or will just a few do?" a man was saying.

A disgusted snort. A woman's voice: "Why would we use some of the bones?"

"God made Eve from one of Adam's ribs," the man said. "He did not need to use the whole skeleton."

"Are you God? I do not think so. You are an old man wearing Greek underpants, so you will need the whole skeleton."

What were they doing? And why hadn't I brought police backup? Even Constable Pappas would have been better than my neighbor and a half-baked dwarf.

"It's definitely not hell," I said to Lydia. "I suspect it's something much worse. It sounds like a bunch of senior citizens trying to cook my grandmother."

I killed and pocketed the flashlight and jumped down the final step, landing squarely in the cavern. It wasn't a massive space. In fact, I'd call it almost cozy, except for the absent windows and the dirt-crusted coffin sitting on a stone altar in the middle. There was a second stone altar beside it, currently bare. Off to the side, a wide, deep fire pit provided warmth and light. The missing senior citizens —Yiayia's friends and body thieves—were all present and accounted for, except for the two ghosts from my apartment. The way they were bustling around, it was like they were getting ready to make a party. Everyone had a job to do. Some were stoking the fire. Eugenia Droulia, Yiayia's lifelong frenemy, was leafing through a hefty book that I suspected was probably an overdue item from the long-lost library of Alexandria. I wondered if it was one of the books on Popi's list. Near Kyria Eugenia's elbow sat a second tome of unknown age. Bound in worn leather, it matched the description of the library's missing logbook.

"Making a party, are we?" I said in a loud, clear voice.

The nice thing about this pack of senior citizens was that their hearing wasn't what it used to be. Sneaking up on them had been a breeze. I had to wave my arms to get their attention. Once they realized I was there, they all jumped.

"Party?" I repeated in a louder voice.

Kyria Eugenia slammed the book shut. "What is she doing here, eh? Who forgot to lock the doors?"

"You were the last one down," Manolis Psaris, vineyard owner, said. "We were carrying the coffin."

How they got Yiayia's coffin down was a mystery. All that potential osteoporosis. One slip and they'd have been a pile of bones at the bottom of the steps.

Kyria Eugenia whipped off her slipper, launched it at his head. Psaris ducked. The slipper landed in the fire and went up in a *whoof* of flames. Kyria Eugenia's forehead crumpled until the skin looked like a topological map of Meteora.

"Now I only have one shoe," she said. "People will think I am poor."

"Half poor," the winemaker said. "You still have one shoe."

Kyria Eugenia turned on me. "Get out."

"Aww, but I just got here, and this looks like a family affair. That is, after all, my grandmother."

"You cannot have her," she said.

I folded my arms. "Neither can you."

"We already have her."

I made a face. "Does anybody ever really have anybody? It's like that old English-language saying: If you love something, set it free. If it comes back it's yours. If it doesn't, it never was."

"There is a better Greek saying: You may as well try to shave an egg." On that note, Kyria Eugenia took off her other slipper and launched it at my head. I ducked. Lydia did, too. The slipper ricocheted off Jimmy's scalp and landed in the fire. It went up in flames like its match.

"Now you look completely poor," Manolis Psaris said.

"Why are you doing this?" I asked them. "And can you even do this … whatever it is you're trying to do? Is it a ritual? Is it a spell? Science?"

"We made a promise to your grandmother that after her death we would bring her back to life," Kyria Eugenia said.

"But why?"

"Because she made us promise to do this thing for her. She was afraid to die, so she made sure she would not be dead for too long."

The math wasn't adding up. Was this algebra? Was it geometry? Who knew? Not me.

"Why now? Why not after her funeral? Why not a year ago? Why not as soon as she passed?" My list of question was long and getting longer by the second. "She would have been fresh then. Now she's goopy. Maybe she's even bones, I don't know."

"It depends on whether or not they embalmed her," Lydia said. The younger woman sounded cool and calm, but her eyes were popping out of their sockets. Spanking men hadn't prepared her for resurrecting the dead.

Manolis Psaris answered. "We cannot bring her back in her body, but we need her body to work the magic to tether her to this world."

"So … you're bringing her ghost back?" I asked.

He didn't look sure about this—any of this. "I think so.

That is what we are doing, yes?"

"That seems weird and probably not possible," I said.

Was I sure? I was not. There was a whole world of supernatural weirdness out there, and I existed on a teeny, tiny pinpoint. Maybe they could call up Yiayia's ghost and keep her here. But that wasn't living. Something about this reeked to high heaven, and it wasn't just this stinky, old cavern with its stale air and dirty, damaged coffin.

"How would you know?" Kyria Eugenia said. "You are a child."

"I know things," I said. "Why would you make this crazy promise to Yiayia? And do you have any proof? A contract? Something more solid than your word? You stole her body. That means your word is pretty much *kaka*."

"We had to wait until your parents were gone on their trip," Manolis Psaris told me.

Wow. He was a fount of information.

"*Vlakas*," Kyria Sugenia said, calling him stupid. "That is not why."

"It was part of it," he said sulkily.

"A lucky coincidence. We had to wait," she told me, "until after Vicki Niki's's hip operation."

Vicki Niki was Vicki Nikopoulous, another one of Yiayia's old crew. If Yiayia was the town motorcycle, by her own admission, Vicki Niki was the scooter. You didn't get very far with her, and you had to do too much pushing with your feet. She'd wanted to be Yiayia, except the job was already taken.

"Two hips. Brand new." Vicki Niki thrust her hips suggestively. Vicki Niki was born the same year as Yiayia. She was skinnier, wrinklier, and she always smelled like garlic. She'd never married, which meant she'd never lost a husband, so she wore any colors she liked. The colors she liked were eye-searing pinks and violent greens, usually in the same outfit. Vicki Niki had been wearing her hair in a massive bouffant for decades now and wasn't about to quit any time soon.

"Mama mia," Jimmy said. "Oh-la-la."

A vein was starting to throb in my temple. "Why?" I asked Kyria Eugenia.

"Because we are going to put Foutoula in her body, and we could not do that with Vicki Niki's bad hips."

"Is this a weird sex thing?" I asked. "Because this really sounds like a weird sex thing."

"All sex is weird when it involves your grandparents," Lydia said beside me.

"She's right," I said. "I mean, it's good that grandparents have sex. But I don't want to know about it when it's mine." I pressed down on the pounding vein. "Okay, party is over. Yiayia goes back in the ground and you all go back to yelling about politics and gossiping about your neighbors. I bet I can even talk my sister out of pressing charges."

No. No, I couldn't. Toula was going to want blood. But they didn't need to know that.

"We made a promise," Manolis Psaris said.

"Promises can be broken, especially when they involve dead people who are no longer hanging around," I told him. "You can't just put people in other people's bodies. We're not built for that, and it's not nice."

Vicki Niki raised her hand. "But I volunteered."

Virgin Mary. These people. "Why?"

"Foutoula was more fun than I am."

"You're fun. You do …" I scrounged around for a lifeline "…needlepoint. You bake things. I see you sweeping all the time. Sweeping looks like fun."

Her face fell. "It is not fun."

"It is to me," I said. "I live in an apartment and I never

get to sweep my yard. We all want what others have. That's human nature."

"But men flocked to Foutoula," Vicki Niki said.

There went that vein again. "Yes, and she practically lived at the doctor because of the urinary tract infections."

"She did stick a lot of yogurt up her *mouni*," Kyria Eugenia pointed out. "A waste of good yogurt if you ask me."

Behind me, Jimmy snickered. "Sometimes I stick my *poutsa* in a tub of yogurt. It helps the chaffing."

Lydia raised an eyebrow at me. I raised one back.

"Can you go back up and call the police?" I asked her. "Take Jimmy with you. If he offers you yogurt, say no."

There was a noise. A dangerous noise. A noise of a dozen slippers sliding off their feet. There was another sound, too, brighter and more dangerous. Someone had brought a rifle to this party. Greece wasn't a country of guns. If you owned one you had to have a good reason. Wanting one? Not considered a good reason. Second Amendment rights? Not a reason. Also, wrong country. Hordes of wild boars? We had bores and pigs but no boars. Protection? Get a mother-in-law, not a gun.

"Run," I yelped and shoved Lydia and Jimmy at the steps. They took off. I landed on my face. "Ow."

The rifle appeared under my nose.

"Stand up," Manolis Psaris said.

"Nice gun. Where did you get it?"

"It was your grandmother's."

"Yiayia owned a gun?" This was news to me, and probably everyone else in my family. "Where did she get it?"

"Payment for service rendered."

"What does that mean?"

"She was sleeping with a politician," he told me. "The

permit was one of the perks."

"She got a lot of perks," Vicky Niki said. "I never got perks. I really want perks."

The rifle's barrel nudged my nose. "Get up. I think that is what I am supposed to say. Did I sound convincing?"

"Totally," I assured the vineyard owner.

"Thank you. I feel better now."

I untangled my limbs and rose slowly from the floor. Manolis Psaris' hands shook. Early Parkinson's or uncertainty? I hoped it was the second thing. "Do you really think you should be the one holding the gun?"

"Why?"

I tilted my chin up then down. "No reason."

His hands continued shaking. "Is it my illness?"

"No."

"She is making fun of my illness," he told the others.

Oh, brother. This was what I got for trying to unravel mysteries. I should have backed off and let Pappas do his police thing instead of trying to find Yiayia myself. At least Pappas had a gun and a badge and backup he could call if he encountered a dozen old folks holed up in a dodgy cavern.

"I wasn't!" I said in my defense.

"He shakes because he is a *malakas*," Papayiannis said.

"That just makes it easier," Manolis Psaris said. "You are just jealous."

"Quick," Kyria Eugenia said. "Put her on the fire!"

Behind them, a handful of Yiayia's pals hoisted up the coffin and carried it over to the fire.

"Stop!" I yelled.

Spoiler alert: They didn't stop. They dumped Yiayia's coffin on top of the blazing fire. Flames licked the tarnished wood along the sides, looking for signs of weakness. The wood was damp. All that fire and moisture created pythons of smoke that snaked out in every direction.

Kyria Eugenia began to read from the book in Ancient Greek. Modern and Ancient Greek were kissing cousins, but she may as well have been speaking Chinese.

The cavern began to fill up with smoke.

"We have to get out of here," I said.

Nobody heard me.

Kyria Eugenia barked more instructions in a booming voice. "Vicky Niki, get up on the altar."

Vicky Niki and her new hips hobbled over to the second stone altar. She stepped up and stripped off. Gravity went wild, grabbing at everything it could get its paws on. I looked away. Gravity was the universe's mean girl. Eventually it would come for me, too. I hoped to have solid foundation garments in my wardrobe by then. Duct tape, too.

But it was possible gravity wouldn't get a shot at me. The cavern was filling up fast. All these old people. All this smoke. A gun in my face.

"Put that stupid thing down." I slapped the rifle out of Manolis Psaris's quaking hands and tucked it under my arm. "You have to get out of here—all of you!"

I used my best outside voice so everyone would get the memo.

"But the ritual," Psaris said. "We promised."

"Do you want to die down here?"

"Good point."

Some of the old folks ditched their stations and began hobbling toward the steps. That's when the carnage started.

Greek society comes with certain rules for survival. Near the top of the list: Never try to board a bus before an elderly Greek woman. The oldest, most decrepit and disabled Greek women—bonus danger if she's a widow—transforms into a superhuman when a bus rattles to a stop. When stink-eyes and casting aspersions about your legitimacy don't work, they get physical. Elbows jab. Feet kick. If you're lucky, you'll have enough life in you to drag your damaged carcass onto the bus behind them.

The narrow and endless steps were the underground equivalent of a bus. The senior citizens went *300* on the invisible Persians, tussling and stomping on each other. War broke out. Cries echoed in the cavern.

Friends? Ha. This wasn't Sparta—it was Merope.

Yup, we were all going to die down here.

Over on the fire pit, Yiayia's coffin ramped up its smoke production. The fire was slowly suffocating. Too much damp wood.

Kyria Eugenia paused her chanting.

"This is fine," she said. "This is normal."

She went back to babbling in Ancient Greek.

"Are you sure you're doing that right?" I called out.

She flipped me off with both hands.

"Is that a yes or a no? I can't tell."

She doubled over, coughed, went back to her ritual.

"Some backup would be great right now," I muttered to myself.

Since backup wasn't happening anytime soon, and war was happening on the steps, it was up to me to save all these fruitcakes. Criminal masterminds or not, I couldn't let them die. They were Merope's elders. I respected them even if they were several nuts short of baklava.

I dug in my bag for a water bottle and poured it on my scarf. I wrapped that around my face. The air wasn't much cleaner but it helped. My eyes stung and watered. I wiped tears away as I dragged Vicky Niki down from the altar. Something cracked. I hoped it wasn't her new hips. I crouched down and threw her over my shoulder, fireman style. Her generation of women weren't built large, and because they'd grown up poor they skipped things like the daily recommended allowance of calcium. So it was like hoisting a feather pillow. I dumped her on the steps with the rest of the old folks, who had given up fighting and were now arguing at the top of their lungs about whose feet hurt the most.

Kyria Eugenia was the last holdout. She chanted. She waved her arms. She flipped me off again when she saw me approaching.

"If we don't go now you'll die down here," I said.

"I have to finish the ritual!"

"No—no ritual. Yiayia is dead. It was sad, yes, but it was her time. You can't just bring her back."

"Yes, ritual!"

I snatched the book, slammed it shut. Now I had a gun and a spell book. Groovy.

"If you die bringing her back then she'll have no friends, anyway."

"We were never friends, except when we were."

Now wasn't the time to analyze her logic for flaws. I grabbed her sinewy arm with my free hand. "We have to go now or die, and I really don't want to die."

She hacked up an invisible hairball, then spat on the ground three times. "You are too late! The ritual is done. Foutoula is coming back!"

With superhuman old lady strength, she wrenched her arm away and ran at the blazing coffin. She leaped on top, hugged the coffin like a starfish. Her perm went up in flames. The stink of keratin filled the cavern as she screamed.

Virgin Mary. When old Greeks believed, they believed *hard*.

Coughing, I helped myself to her ankle, dragging until she fell off the coffin and onto the ground. With what was left of my energy reserves, I hauled her over to the steps and stomped on her hair until it was nothing more than a smoking mess.

"Go," I said, breathlessly. The smoke poked its fingers through the scarf. Every breath was at least fifty percent carcinogens and a disturbing amount of Yiayia's coffin.

Coughing and spluttering, the last of Merope's senior citizens began to climb. My work here was done. They'd be safe. And bonus: I'd found Yiayia, even if she was currently the subject of the world's slowest cremation.

Empty, I flopped down on the bottom step. A tiny nap was just the ticket. Then I'd have energy to make the climb. Right? Right.

It was a sloppy lie, but it was the only one I was capable of forming.

"You are dying," the Man in Black said. He crouched down beside me, pulled the scarf from my mouth.

"You're here," I said.

"Sometimes."

"Am I really dying?"

"Yes."

"I'd really like to not do that."

"Are you sure?"

"Positive. My sister would be mad, and there's cheese in my refrigerator. I'd hate to waste it."

He picked me up. I'd like to say it felt romantic in a man-striding-across-the-moors-in-a-movie way, but dying sucks all the innocent romance out of situations. The one time an escapee from an Austen book saves me and I couldn't even enjoy it.

Instead, my head fell back. My lungs stopped working. And I died.

CHAPTER THIRTEEN

The Afterlife looked a lot like the ICU in Merope's hospital. Probably because it was the ICU in Merope's hospital and not the Afterlife at all. I tried cheering but the tube in my throat was a real party pooper.

I wasn't dead. Hooray.

A nurse hurried over. She wasn't alone. Leo was there, too. Tears in his eyes and everything.

"You're okay," he said.

I gave him a thumbs up, then tried to remember if it was on Greece's obscene gesture list. In my current condition I couldn't recall, so I put the thumb away.

"Don't talk," he said, as though I could. He planted himself in the chair next to the bed. "You managed to save everyone, including yourself. We've got a dozen of the island's senior citizens on oxygen right now, too, and Eugenia Droulia is being treated for burns. From what I can tell, they got it into their heads to perform some kind of ritual to bring your grandmother back from the dead." He made a face like they were insane—which they kind of were. But they were old and their hobbies were pretty bland, so I couldn't blame them for trying to spice things up. "Jimmy and Lydia called the moment they got a signal. Pappas and I found you passed out about halfway up. Another minute and there would have been no bringing you back." His voice cracked. "Toula doesn't know yet."

"Toula knows," Toula said from the doorway in a voice that suggested balls were about to be on the chopping block. Any balls that happened to be in the vicinity. Even balls she used to enjoy. "What did I tell you about almost dying?" She glared down at me. "Don't. Do. It."

"She found your grandmother's remains," Leo said.

Toula whipped out her pointer finger. She stuck it right up under his nose. "Do I look like I give a shit about my dead grandmother?" she barked at him. "My sister almost died. Yiayia was already dead."

I waved my hands at them. I wanted to be part of this discussion but the tube was really cramping my style and ability to argue.

"Anyway, why was Allie doing police work? When someone steals something, that's a law enforcement thing, not a civilian thing."

"Allie did this on her own," Leo said. "With my cousin and her neighbor."

I rocked my hand side to side.

"And Constable Pappas," Leo added. "Who wasn't there at the time because he was helping me with a homicide."

The air whooshed out of my sister. She fell into the other chair.

"This can't happen again," she said.

"I agree," Leo said. "So do we take turns locking Allie in her apartment?"

"We could get her a big crate. Dogs love crates. Allie might, too."

I glared at them as hard as I could, flat on my back, with a tube stuck down my throat. It wasn't easy but I'd like to say I succeeded in slapping them both with my best stink-eye.

A nurse bustled in with a couple of medical sidekicks. "You're stable, so we're going to get that tube out and see if you can breathe on your own, okay?"

"Can we put her in a crate afterwards?" my sister asked.

The nurse looked at me. "You can try."

———

The doctor wanted to keep me overnight. Since it was three in the morning, I rolled with that. By the time breakfast—bread and cheese—appeared, I was dressed in my regular clothes and pacing. My throat hurt and my voice sounded like it had been dragged over broken glass, but I was fine. Really.

"Don't you think you should stay a bit longer," Leo said.

"Let me think about it … No."

"Smoke inhalation is dangerous."

"I know, which is why I want to leave. Too much secondhand smoke in my hair."

"At least come and stay at my place for a couple of days so I can keep an eye on you."

"You do realize I live directly beneath you, right?"

He smiled. "Indulge me."

"And share a drawer with Jimmy? I don't think so."

"You can sleep in my bed."

I flushed. If I was in Leo's bed I wouldn't be sleeping. Not at first, anyway. And right now I really, really wanted to sleep. "Let's schedule that sleepover for another time," I rasped.

Leo didn't look happy. "Keep your phone with you all the time. If you don't answer a text right away I'm calling an ambulance."

"Melodramatic."

"You almost died."

"And yet here I am." I thought about it for a moment. "Was there anyone else down there?"

"In the cavern? No. All we found were your grand-mother's remains. Fekkas will rebury her later."

What had happened to the Man in Black? He came and went as he pleased. But he'd saved my life, that much was true.

"Her coffin didn't burn to a crisp?"

"The fire ran out of oxygen before there was too much damage. The casket was barely singed."

I closed my eyes. I didn't believe the ritual was going to bring back anything, least of all Yiayia, but it was nice to know it was a big fat failure.

"I want to be there when Fekkas reburies her," I said. "To make sure nothing goes wrong."

"Fekkas can do it without you. He knows how to do his job. You're going home to rest."

The idea appealed to me. A day on the couch with television and Dead Cat was exactly what the doctor ordered.

"One day on the couch," I said, lying through my teeth, although I didn't know it yet.

———

On the way out of the hospital, I stopped to check on

Yiayia's friends, who were still under observation for a number of maladies, including smoke inhalation and sore feet. One of Vicky Niki's legs had snapped when I dragged her off the altar, and Kyria Eugenia's hair would grow back again someday maybe, if the scar tissue wasn't too bad.

None of them looked happy to see me.

"You are alive," Kyria Eugenia said through lips that looked like bubble wrap when I reached her room.

"Surprise. I'm alive and Yiayia's not."

"That is what you think," she said darkly.

I gestured toward Vicky Niki's room, where her broken leg was all propped up in plaster. "She's still herself. I know my grandmother and that's not her."

"Then Foutoula went somewhere else."

"Why did you do it?"

"Foutoula was my best friend and worst enemy. Without her I have no one to love or hate. You would not understand."

"So you pulled a ritual out of a book? What made you think that was going to work? It's like a recipe book. The recipes sound yummy and the pictures make it look like the best food ever, but when it comes to the cooking something's just not quite right."

"It has worked before, for others."

"When?"

Her gaze darted away.

"I do not know."

"So then how did you know it would work?"

"It was in a book."

"Books are filled with all kinds of things that aren't true. Same with movies. People like stories because they could be real but they're not."

"You know nothing."

"I know Yiayia didn't magically come back to life in Vicky Niki's body."

"Yet."

———

Leo followed me into my apartment. All was quiet across the hall. No sign of Lydia.

"Is she okay?" I asked.

"She was worried about you, but she and Jimmy are fine." His forehead sprouted new lines. "What was with the goats last night?"

"Snoozing. Goats adore naps, and it was night."

His eyebrows took a hike. "Really?"

"I know nothing," I said in a tone that suggested I knew everything but wasn't about to pony up my secret sources. Cannabis was illegal around these parts, and I didn't want Jimmy to get into trouble, even if he was a human mosquito.

When I left the hospital, it was with the books and without the rifle. The police confiscated the gun, seeing as how the last person to have a license for it was Yiayia. I was okay with that. I was more interested in the books anyway. Tomorrow I'd return the logbook to the library. Probably I'd keep the spell book, until I found it a good home. It was old. Somewhere out there was a collector of ancient and arcane books with spells and rituals that maybe didn't work. While I considered giving the book to Betty—she knew more woo-woo people—Leo moved from room to room like he was hunting for bad guys.

"Everything okay?" I asked him.

"Let me be paranoid. It's the least I can do since I can't be here to watch you."

"I'll be fine, I promise."

Everything was exactly where I'd left it, except the little pink jar had rolled off the table. I sat it on the table and vowed to have a one-sided conversation with Dead Cat about knocking stuff off the coffee table. No doubt he'd ignore me, maintaining the human-cat status quo.

Leo kissed me, long and deep. My toes tingled. Then I coughed, breaking the spell.

"Go," I said, with a smoke-shredded voice.

"I'll be back."

"Bring food."

"Crusty Dimitri's?"

"I said food, not toxic waste."

He closed the door, and I locked it behind him.

Five minutes later, I was in the shower, washing the night out of my hair. My phone pinged. I reached out to check. Message from Alfred, Angela's butler. He wanted to know if I'd found her yet.

Angela.

Yiayia's post-mortem abduction had thrown a spanner into my plans. Now that her shot at seizing control of Vicky Niki's body was over, new hips and all, I could refocus on my efforts to find Angela. Shower first. Then the Cake Emporium's shortcut to the UK.

"Did they do it?"

I jumped. The shampoo leaped out of my hand. Lather ran into my eyes. I squealed.

Yiorgos Dakis and Konstantinos Grivas were back—both of them—and they were in my bathroom.

"Get out!"

They looked at each other and shrugged. "Like we have not seen a naked woman before," Dakis said. "I was seeing naked women before you were born."

"You were eighty-years-old before you died, so I should hope so," I said. "Otherwise you were stunted."

Grivas snickered. "She called you stunted."

"She can call me anything she likes as long as she does not get dressed."

Eww, eww, eww. I snatched the towel off the rack and wrapped myself from neck to knee. "Get out or I'll call the Ghostbusters. They're women now. That means they seriously won't tolerate *kaka*."

"We just want to know if the ritual worked," Dakis said.

"No, the ritual didn't work. There was fire and a lot of smoke and then a lot of nothing. Everyone is in the hospital, so maybe you should go there."

"We already went but they cannot see us. I do not suppose you could help us talk to Eugenia?" Dakis did puppy dog eyes. I wasn't falling for that.

"No."

"Foutoula would have helped us," he said.

Ha. Not in a million years. Yiayia was a lot of things but she wasn't nuts, which was why it was hard to believe she'd ever pushed anyone to promise they'd bring her back from the dead. "She would have told you to jump in a lake."

"After she had violated our bodies," he said.

I shuddered. Nobody needed that mental image, especially not when the circumstances of his accidental death were fresh in my mind. "Go away. I have somewhere to be."

"The policeman told you to stay here," Konstantinos Grivas said.

"You've been eavesdropping again?"

"We are dead, what else do you expect us to do with our time?"

"Dead people stuff." I wrapped my hair in a second towel. "Move on and experience a rich, full Afterlife."

"We cannot move on," Dakis said.

"I was murdered, remember?" Grivas said. "And he cannot move on because he has unfinished business."

Good point. "What is your unfinished business anyway?"

"I wish I could remember," Yiorgos Dakis said forlornly.

"Well, I have to go, no matter what the policeman says."

Ten minutes later I was back on my bicycle and wheeling toward the Cake Emporium. I was moving slowly on account of how almost dying from smoke inhalation really does a number on your lungs. Clouds of steam formed around my face as I leaned my bicycle outside the confectionary store. I inhaled through my nose, exhaled slowly.

As I stepped into the Cake Emporium world, Betty rushed toward me and enfolded me in her arms. The scent of vanilla and strawberries surrounded me.

"I heard about your troubles," she said. "I'm so glad you're okay. I knew you would be, but I'm relieved all the same. I take it you're here for that trip to Merry Old England? Are you sure you're up to it, love? I know your policeman would rather you stay put. He's one of the good ones."

"It's just a little meet-and-greet, basically."

The plan was to talk to Sir Teddy Duckworth, face to face. If that didn't work out, I'd dig out my old theater skills and improvise.

She winked and began bustling around behind the counter. "And little pink piggies fly. But as long as you're feeling okay, my portal is your portal. I should have said that in Spanish. Everything sounds prettier in a foreign language." She presented me with a white paper bag. "A little something for the trip. You need to keep your strength up."

I peeked inside. "Marzipan animals?"

"Marzipan is just almonds, and almonds are a popular health food."

Her generosity humbled me. Somehow I was surrounded by good people, and Betty Honeychurch was one of the best.

"If there's anything I can ever do for you …"

"You already did, didn't you? You released Jack and me from being trapped in our own house for all eternity, and you give the gift of friendship every day. Now come along." She led me into the kitchen, and out through another door, and then through the Honeychurch house's French doors. Betty's beloved childhood dog Duchess was waiting, wagging her tail. I gave the wolfhound a pet neither of us could feel. Death didn't stop me wanting to hug all the dogs. Hopefully Dead Cat would never discover my betrayal.

I was surrounded by luxury. Betty and Jack's mansion was fit for royalty. A person could ride a bicycle up and down the hallways and never touch the walls. The art was the oddest thing about the house … besides the portal to the Cake Emporium. Paintings and sculptures from artists who didn't exist in my time or world, who didn't create using materials I understood. Some of the more obscure paintings hurt my eyes. They didn't make sense to my brain. By the time we reached the tall, ornately carved front doors, my eyes were crossed.

There was a car waiting out front. Not just any car. A Jaguar. Classic Sherwood Green paint.

"Thank you," I said.

"You're doing us a favor, aren't you? Jack tells me that the mechanical things will go wonky if it just sits in the garage. Best thing is for you to take it out to stretch its legs."

"I'll take good care of it."

"You'll find it'll take even better care of you. Oops. Someone's coming to the shop. Got to go."

With a wink, she bustled back into her mansion.

The Jaguar was gorgeous but intimidating. It was like standing in front of a king or queen and not knowing whether to curtsey or treat them like a regular human being. The car was unlocked. The keys were in the ignition. Probably there weren't a lot of car thieves wandering around the English countryside.

I angled in. The seat had been adjusted to accommodate my unremarkable height. The mirrors were angled so that I could see most of the world around me. The Jaguar came to life as I turned the key. A low, civilized growl.

My phone told me to take a left out of the Honeychurch property, so that's what I did.

The day was gray, with low-hanging clouds that threatened rain but never produced more than a half-hearted drop. The clouds made the world feel smaller, more confined, as though England were a room and not a country. Merope was a rock in the middle of the Aegean Sea. Cast a gaze over any edge and the world seemed infinite.

For a moment I couldn't breathe. What was I thinking? I should have stayed home like I promised Leo.

The temperature in the Jaguar dropped. Cold air rushed at my face. I took deep gasps, and the world began to open up again.

I was fine the rest of the way.

After the emptiness of Merope, the city was downright intimidating. So much traffic. Too many people. Buildings pressed up against each other. No space went uninvaded. Sir Teddy Duckworth lived in a middle class neighborhood on the outskirts, where houses barely touched and everything that wasn't brown or orange brick was white paint. Fences were high. Garages, if they were present, were tiny compared to their American counterparts. Merope didn't have garages. Not enough cars. Half the houses were built when donkey was the only mode of transportation beyond feet.

Sir Teddy Duckworth worked in construction, so I expected no one home—there was no Mrs. Duckworth, according to my research—but I rang the doorbell anyway.

Predictably, no one answered.

The neighborhood felt empty. People on Merope were always outside if the weather permitted. How else could they mind everyone else's business? If the British were snooping on their neighbors, they were doing it from behind their sheer curtains.

Sir Teddy Duckworth didn't have curtains. He was a Venetian blinds kind of guy. They covered every angle of the shallow bay window downstairs. Unlike curtains, blinds left gaps. I tried to look cute, perky, and as though there was nothing weird about me craning my neck this way and that to get a look inside. If the neighbors were peeping from behind their lacy sheers, hopefully they'd spot the Jaguar first and assume I was respectable, or at least not a thief.

From what I could see, Duckworth favored vanilla walls and brown furniture from a bygone era, when Jell-O was considered a legitimate salad ingredient and people bought appliances in colors like avocado. The bookshelves downstairs held model castles, the very thing that had attracted Angela to Sir Teddy in the first place. Her experiences in the adult portion of her life had taught her that when a man said he owned a castle, he meant one she could live in and keep after the divorce. The part of Angela that had

grown up dirt poor kept me around because she was naturally suspicious of everyone, especially if they claimed to
own castles. Technically Sir Teddy Duckworth hadn't been
lying about his castles. But like many a man, he'd exagger-
ated about size.

No signs of Angela. Or any woman. From what I could
see, which wasn't much, the place was thoroughly
masculine.

What now? I stood on the sidewalk (or was it called a
pavement here?) and considered my next move.

The curtains across the street twitched.

A sign. Or at least I decided to take it that way.

I crossed over the narrow street and knocked on the
door of a house almost identical to its neighbors.

"Are you collecting money for some kind of charity
then?" a voice said through the mail slot in the door.

"Not today. My name is Allie Callas, and I'm looking
for someone."

"What kind of someone? Are you one of them
foreigners?"

"I'm Greek-American."

"Steal anyone's job lately?"

"I'm self-employed in another country."

"What do you think of Brexit?"

"I try not to. The whole thing gives me a headache."

The door opened. Sir Teddy Duckworth's nosy
neighbor was a Q-Tip in a flat cap. His face said he had
blood pressure issues, and his purple nose said his favorite
sport was raising a beer can. He had seven decades crossed
on his bingo card and was working on the eighth.

"What's that fookin' fool done now?"

"Sir Teddy Duckworth?"

"Sir, my fookin' arse. What kind of name is that? He's
above himself, that one. Go on then, what did he do?"

"I'm not sure he did anything. I'm looking for a friend of mine. Last I heard she was coming to visit Duckworth, then she vanished."

"A lot of women come to visit that one. They show up a few times then they never come back. They're like chips to a man like that. There's always more of them at the shop, and they're always hot."

I showed him a photograph of Angela on my phone. "This is my friend."

He nodded. "A-yep. I saw her the other day. Showed up in a fancy limousine. The driver dropped her off and left. Good legs on her. Nice arse, too. Never did see her leave, come to think of it. And I was here all night, too."

"Are you here a lot?"

"Cheaper than a television license, watching the neighborhood. Most of the neighbors are boring, but there's a few like Duckworth who make it worthwhile. Him and those castles he builds. He's always loading up the newest one, taking it to some show or another. Fancies himself as a real artist. It's a bit bloody poncy if you ask me, making castles. That's right up there with knitting and that thing women do where they stab material a bunch of times, only to wind up making something you couldn't pay a person to accept as a present."

He was thoroughly charming, in a raw, unfinished way.

"So Angela came and never left. Is there anything else you can tell me about Duckworth, Mr. …"

"Charlie Brown. You can call me Charlie. Mister makes me feel old. I'm not ready to feel old. I suspect I won't be until my time is up."

"Charlie," I said, not making any *Peanuts* jokes or asking after Snoopy. "Was there ever a Mrs. Duckworth?"

"Mavis. His mother. She used to live with him until he had her put into one of those homes to rot. Never would tell me which one. She and I were friendly, so I thought about visiting. Sir Arsehole said his mother was losing her marbles and it would be better for her if I stayed away."

"Any idea where he is right now?"

"Working on some building or another. Give it a few minutes and he'll be home for lunch. He always comes home to eat. He's a real cheapskate except when it comes to his castles. You can wait here if you like. Got a good view of his yard."

"Thanks, but I have to send some emails," I said.

"Suit yourself," he said. "If he happens to blab about where his mum is, let me know, will you?"

I promised I'd do exactly that, and went back to the Jaguar to check my emails. A text message had arrived moments ago from Leo, wanting me to confirm that I was still alive. I wrote back that I was and he sent me a smiley face. Good thing he didn't ask *where* I was alive. There was a text from Toula demanding to know what I was doing. I told her I was on the toilet, and that seemed to mollify her. She wrote that Christos Fekkas was scheduled to put Yiayia back in the ground, where she belonged, later this afternoon. I had several new Finders Keepers emails, basic requests I managed to fulfill within minutes, using the power of the internet.

I sent Sam a message, asking if Angela's phone was still at the Duckworth house. He wrote back almost immediately, confirming that the cell phone's new living situation was unchanged.

Fear gave my gut a firm squeeze. I wanted Angela to be okay.

Not fifteen minutes later, an older BMW rolled into the street and turned in to Sir Teddy Duckworth's driveway. Sir Teddy got out a moment later. He looked like his pictures. Boyishly attractive, in a plain, sandy-haired way.

A ham and cheese sandwich on white bread of a man—hold the mustard. Too short for his weight. His work boots were dusty and his pants reveled several centimeters of hirsute crack. He performed a double take when he spotted the Jaguar, but it didn't hold his interest for long.

I jumped out, ignoring my slight shortness of breath.

"Sir Teddy Duckworth?"

That stopped him in his tracks. "What's it to you?"

"We spoke on the phone. I'm looking for Angela Zouboulaki."

"Never heard of her, except last time you called looking for her."

"That's hard to believe, seeing as how eyewitnesses saw her here."

"Was she now?" His gaze cut across the street. "Can't imagine where you heard that. I don't know what to tell you. She never knocked on my door, that's all I know."

"She told me herself that she was coming here to see you."

"Well then she's a crazy person, because I don't know any Angela."

He was lying. He was so very much lying. And he stank at it. His cheeks went from pale to purple. His gaze bounced around like a jalopy down a dirt road. He knew Angela. I'd bet his life on it.

"Let me show you a picture."

He sighed like I was killing him but made a hurry-up motion with his hands. I shoved my phone under his nose. He glanced at the screen.

"Still don't know her."

"Well, okay," I said.

I hopped in the Jaguar and drove around the corner. I got out, jumped the fence, and knocked on Charlie Brown's back door.

The door flew open. "Well? Did you find your friend?"

"He hasn't seen her," I said.

"What did I tell you? That's a fookin' liar, that one."

"He really is a fookin' liar," I said. "And I really need to take a peek inside his house."

Charlie ushered me inside. "Got something for you. Been saving it for a rainy day or in case the cops came by and wanted to search the Duckworth place for bodies buried under the floorboards."

His furnishings were from the same era as Sir Teddy Duckworth's, but with more cabbage roses and the overwhelming scent of menthol. He lifted the lid on a small china container sitting on a sideboard and presented me with a shiny key.

"Front door," he said. "Mavis and I swapped keys in case one of us fell down and couldn't get up."

"Smart," I said.

"You go on in there once he leaves and take a good look around. If you can, you find out where his mum is and you let me know. I'd like to see her again before it's too late."

CHAPTER FOURTEEN

SIR TEDDY DUCKWORTH didn't stick around long. Before the hour was up, he wedged himself in his German car and reversed down the driveway.

I gave it five comfortable minutes before I let myself into his place.

Normally trespassing made me feel icky. This wasn't *normally*. Duckworth knew where Angela was—heck, he knew who she was. His lies made my morals about things like breaking and entering (was it "breaking" if I had a key?) flex.

The door closed behind me with a quiet *snick*. Duckworth's place wasn't anything fancy, which I already knew from peeping between his blinds like a common Tom. No art on the walls beyond a Castle of the Month calendar hanging in the hallways, two months behind the times.

Where to begin?

Too bad Sam couldn't narrow down the signal further. Even in a small house there's a hundred places to hide a cell phone. I decided to start in the front room—the living room, by the looks of it. It contained all the usual suspects:

couch, butt-battered recliner, wide-screen TV. Sir Teddy Duckworth was a fan of documentaries about the royal family, according to the stack of DVDs stored in the TV stand.

He was also really, seriously, deeply into his castles. In front of the TV sat a table containing his newest project, an unfinished replica of a castle I vaguely recognized. The plans on the table said it was Lancaster Castle. The name didn't ring a bell but the shape did.

His work was amazing. As I checked out shelves, I marveled at how he'd nailed the tiniest of details. The man was a lying turd, but he knew castles.

The back of my neck prickled.

My head whipped around. I was alone. No ghosts. No impending Sir Teddy. Still, I couldn't shake the feeling someone was watching me. Maybe I was on camera. I hoped not. Talking my way out of video evidence didn't sound like fun.

The sooner I got out of here the better.

I started at one end of the room. A methodical phone hunt commenced. My hope had been to find Angela alive and well with her phone, but that seemed less and less likely.

By the time I reached the bedrooms I had to admit there was nowhere to hide a grown woman. Every potential body-hiding place was filled with arts and crafts supplies. I pawed through paints and tiny but real bricks, bags of miniature rocks and fake grass, hunting for Angela or her phone.

Nothing.

The eyes didn't quit following me. Something was there. I recognized the sensation.

I peered behind books in the guest bedroom's three-shelf bookcase. No phone. Then my attention snagged on one of the titles. I remembered it from Popi's list. Rare. Difficult to acquire, unless a person had access to a pot of gold and a generous leprechaun. Popi and the library didn't know any leprechauns, which was why she unofficially hired me.

My fingers itched. I really, really wanted that book.

But I couldn't do it. I played fair or not at all. Everything I found for people was the result of a trade or reasonable payment. No one walked away feeling cheated. I couldn't just steal. Popi would have to do without *Little People of the Ancient World*. Probably it wouldn't fly off the library's shelf anyway.

Little People wasn't the only strange book in the bookcase. Its nearest neighbors were witchcraft tomes and spell books. Sir Teddy was one eclectic guy.

A key turned in front door's lock.

Heart pumping like a lunatic, I lunged toward the window. While I'd been wrestling with my moral code, Sir Teddy Duckworth had come back for a second lunch or a lengthy rendezvous with his bathroom. Whatever the reason, he was back and here I was, stuck in his house, with nowhere to hide. Not with his arts and crafts habit.

What now?

My attention cut to the windows themselves. Unlike Greek windows, these came with screens. There was no way for me to pop one loose and shimmy out like a common thief. I'd have to find an uncommon thief's way out.

How did Santa handle these situations?

Magic, probably.

I didn't have any of that. The ability to see ghosts and find things wasn't going to save my bacon.

The bed, the little voice inside my head said. I crouched down. Sure enough, there was a space under the bed, next to one of those under-bed storage containers with the wheels. I eased in next to it and tried not to breathe. Not easy when just a few hours earlier I'd been intubated for sucking smoke.

Sir Teddy Duckworth moved around downstairs, making a racket. From the sounds of it he was whipping up a second lunch. A door opened and closed. Not the front door. For the next few minutes there was silence.

All I needed was him gone for two minutes so I could flee the scene of the no-actual-crime.

I rested my head on my folded arms and waited.

My gaze was drawn to the container beside me.

Everything else in the house seemed to be related to Sir Teddy's castle obsession. Not this plastic container. This looked like a bits and pieces drawer, where stray cables and other random, homeless objects came to hide out, until their owner remembered he needed them. Every home had something like it. A drawer, usually. My junk drawer was in my desk. Everything that didn't belong wound up there. Twist-ties. Rubber bands. A rock Milos gave me. One of Patra's biggest boogers. Those little wrenches that come with furniture these days, because furniture never arrives whole unless you know a guy who handcrafts furniture or you have deep pockets. Even in Greece, carpenters were dying out, replaced by do-it-yourself retailers.

My attention snagged on a pattern amongst the container's chaos.

A cell phone. No—more than one. There were several distinct outlines. At least half a dozen. Was one of them Angela's? To whom did the others belong? Why did Sir Teddy Duckworth have a plastic container full of phones?

None of the potential answers were good.

One ear on the silence downstairs, I tried to work my

fingers into the container without making a sound. Plastic bit into my hand. I winced, but I persisted.

One of the phones lit up. It began to play that familiar iPhone ring tone. A name and face appeared on the screen. Alfred, Angela's butler, was calling.

Her phone was here. But no Angela.

My fingers jerked back like they'd been burned. The silence downstairs filled with quiet, ominous noise. The floor creaked. The stairs creaked, too.

Sir Teddy Duckworth was coming.

CHAPTER FIFTEEN

I CLOSED my eyes and played dead as he stooped over and rolled the plastic container out. He popped the lid, retrieved the still ringing phone. The phone made a beep as he answered the call. He didn't speak. He just stood there like a psychopath, holding the phone.

At least that's how I imagined it. I couldn't exactly see because I was under the bed with my eyes closed, trying to avoid the reality of my situation. My flight or fight instincts reverted to some weird and previously unknown ancestor. Maybe an ostrich.

"Mrs. Angela?" Alfred said all the way from Greece. "Are you there? Mrs. Angela? Come home. You are needed here. I have no one to cook toast for."

His voice was distant, but even from the under bed and a thousand miles away, something raw and real was evident: Angela's butler was at least a tiny bit in love with her.

"I sent Miss Allie to find you," Alfred went on. "I believe she will stop at nothing to find you and bring you home."

He was right. I'd do whatever it took.

Whatever that was.

Sir Teddy dropped the phone in the container. He closed the lid. With his boot, he shoved the container back under the bed.

A tickle started in my lung.

Not now. Please, not now.

I held my breath. While I was doing that, I felt around in my bag for a backup plan. Pepper spray. The can took a beating the first time I'd encountered the Man in Black. Hopefully it was functional.

A cough blasted out. I tasted smoke.

Uh-oh.

"What the fook?"

Now it was on. The only way to save myself was to be quicker.

On the count of one … two … three …

Pepper spray in hand, I rolled out from under the bed and hit the trigger. Liquid capsaicin and glycol blasted out of the can and into Sir Teddy Duckworth's eyes before he could react to my sudden appearance. I snatched Angela's phone out of his hand and raced down the stairs. My lungs burned. My limbs felt weak. Black dots flickered in my eyes.

Thunder rolled behind me. Thunder or Sir Teddy's work boots.

"You fookin' bitch!" he yelled. "I knew you were up to no good!"

I half skidded, half fell to a stop at the bottom of the stairs, then launched myself at the door. Sir Teddy's meaty fingers closed around my bag's strap. I punched him in the nose with the spray can and whacked his shins with my boot.

He howled. I yanked my bag free and bolted through

the door with Sir Teddy after me.

And there, sitting in the middle of his lawn, was the Jaguar. Not even remotely where I'd left it. The driver's door was open. The engine was purring.

I fell in and hit the gas, hoping like hell it was already in reverse. The car shot backwards into the street, bumping over the curb. Sir Teddy reached for the door handle as I fumbled to get the car into first gear. He jumped back like he'd been bitten.

"Ahhh!" he screamed, shaking his hand. Smoke rose from his fingertips. Looked to me like someone got zapped.

Being Greek, I wasn't prone to looking gift horses in the mouth. I hit the gas and peeled away.

My heart rate didn't return to normal until I reached the local shops, several blocks south. I pulled over and sat with the engine idling, my hands braced on the steering wheel, breathing in through my nose and out through my mouth. The Jaguar blew cool air at my face. Slowly, the black dots disappeared.

My phone buzzed.

—*Everything okay?*

Nurse Leo checking in.

—*Perfect.*

I added a smiley face I didn't feel.

Angela's phone was on the passenger seat. I picked it up. Her butler was still on the line.

"It's Allie," I told him, mildly out of breath. "I found Angela's phone."

"What happened?"

"I'm not sure, but it got weird fast."

"Find her. Please."

I wanted to. I really did. But until I understood what was going on, I couldn't risk going back to Sir Teddy Duckworth's house. Although her phone—and several others—had been in Sir Teddy's possession, there was no sign of Angela or the owners of the other phones. Possibly they were the women Charlie Brown had mentioned. He said they'd come and gone, but did he actually mean he'd witnessed them leaving? I didn't even know who they were or any other useful, pertinent information.

Using Sam's powers for good, I located Charlie Brown's phone number and called him.

"Wowee!" Charlie said. "That was the best afternoon I've had in a long time. Did you see that Duckworth minger jump? What did you do to him anyway?"

"I think my car zapped him with electricity."

"They can do that?"

"Oh sure. Cars these days can do a lot of cool things."

"If I was twenty years younger and could see the road I'd get me one of them. Did you find out anything about his mother?"

"That's what I wanted to ask you—one of the questions, anyway. What's her name? Mavis you said?"

"Mavis Duckworth."

"Is she responsible for naming her son Sir?"

He scoffed. "That was the father. He had airs that one did. Wanted his kid to be royalty."

"Hold tight," I said.

I ended the call and hit my usual databases for information. When they came up empty, I called Sam again.

"Mavis Duckworth? As far as I can tell she's still living with her kid."

"Apparently not," I said. "I was in that house, there's no sign of anyone, let alone his mother."

"Well, someone is collecting her pension, and she's not in any of the country's nursing homes. Maybe the son offed her and stashed the body."

Things like that happened. Sam and I both knew it.

Sinister and sinister-er. Ol' Sir Teddy Duckworth stunk to high heaven. I'd come here looking for information about Angela and instead wound up hip deep in dog *kaka*.

I called Charlie Brown back and told him what Sam had told me.

"He did something to her. I know he did. So what do we do now?"

"Call the police?" I said.

"Call the police, she says. What are the police going to do? Take a look around, find nothing, and leave. I already called the police when Mavis vanished. They told me to buy a telly and watch that instead."

"Wow. The nerve."

"The police are bollocks. They don't do a thing unless there's a scone in it for them."

I asked him about the other women and whether he'd watched them leave. He scratched his head and said now that he thought about it, Angela wasn't the only one who'd come and never left.

There was no way Teddy would leave his house anytime soon, not after today's shenanigans. Without something, some kind of foothold, I had no choice but to go skulking back to Merope. It was getting late. Before I knew it, Leo would be showing up with food—I hoped.

"I'll be in touch," I said. "In the meantime, don't do anything I wouldn't do."

Charlie's voice had a cheeky grin in it. "Give me a list then so I know what I'm working with."

CHAPTER SIXTEEN

AFTER THE JAGUAR'S comfortable ride, my bicycle felt
foreign and flimsy. I loved it anyway. The world was
smaller here on Merope, and I was okay with that. I wasn't
a car person, no matter how nice the car.

In fact, I wasn't a hundred percent sure Betty and
Jack's Jaguar actually was a car. It … wasn't typical. It
zapped Sir Teddy Duckworth and it hadn't sat and stayed
when I told it to. But I was too tired to question Betty
when I stumbled back into the Cake Emporium's kitchen.

She'd handed me a box on the way out and ordered
me home to bed.

I carried the box upstairs. All was still quiet at Lydia's
place. I hoped everything was okay and she'd recovered
from last night. Or was it this morning? Time was starting
to blur—or maybe it was just me. One-handed, I unlocked
the door and nudged it open with my boot-covered toe.

My apartment was full of ghosts. Jam-packed. Border-
line overflowing.

Virgin Mary.

I pulled the door shut. Locked it. Sat on the stairs

between floors and opened Betty's goodie box. She'd filled it with my favorites, including maple éclairs. I selected one and crammed it into my mouth. When that was gone, I moved on to the mille-feuille.

Kid-sized footsteps echoed on the steps, then stopped. "*Mana mou*, I wondered how you giants got so big, and now I know."

I pulled the custard pastry away from my mouth. "Eat a bag of *poutsas*, Jimmy."

"Did that in one of my movies. Decided it wasn't for me. But the money was good. Bought these boots with it, in fact."

He was in his UGGs again. On anyone else they were knee-highs. On Jimmy they were assless chaps.

"Go away," I said. "I'm trying to eat cake. I can't eat cake if you keep talking at me."

With the boots cramping his walking style, he stumped down the next few stairs and took a good look at me. "That's not eating. I know eating. What you're doing is burying your feelings in food."

"Are you a therapist now?"

"I played a therapist in my second movie," he said like being a porn psychologist was an accomplishment. "Tell *baba* what's wrong."

A *baba* was a daddy. Jimmy was not my daddy.

"Eww." I made a face. I went back to cramming pastry into my mouth. It wasn't a solution to the dozens of ghosts in my apartment, but it tasted good. Maybe I could live here on the steps and eat sugar for the rest of my life. As far as life goals went, that wasn't too destructive. At least it wasn't drugs.

"When you're done with that, I have a fresh batch of edibles," Jimmy said.

"No thanks. I saw what your edibles did to goats—and

to you."

"You need to unwind. There's a giant stick up your *kolos*."

"That's just my regular personality when you're around."

Lydia's door opened. She peered out. "Do you have to be so loud? *Skasmos* or you'll get the *koutala*."

The wooden spoon was a good threat, but it was Lydia. She wasn't into spanking women.

"I'm eating cake," I said. "He's the loud one."

"The *nanos*? Half a man, half the manners," she said in a mean, hard voice.

Jimmy's mouth fell open. Mine did, too. A chunk of pastry fell onto my lap. I picked it up and stuffed it back in, my gaze cutting back to Jimmy. His face turned red. He looked down at his boots. He didn't have to look far.

I held the box out to him. "Cake?"

He tilted his chin up then down, and stomped back upstairs. A moment later I heard the small sound of Leo's front door clicking shut.

"What's your problem?" I said to Lydia, who was hovering in the doorway wrapped in a cardigan. It was a change for her. Usually clothing was something she tried to avoid in mass quantities.

She vanished back into her apartment. The door closed.

From where I was sitting—on the steps, with cake—the entire world was on fire. My apartment was full of ghosts. Lydia, who was often prickly but never cruel, had morphed into Toula when she has PMS. And Angela was still missing.

At least Yiayia was where she belonged. That was one thing scrubbed off my to-do list.

My phone buzzed. Leo was checking in on me again.

—What are you doing?

—Eating cake.

—Save some for me.

Ha. Like that was going to happen. I needed this sugar. It wasn't giving me clarity the way caffeine did, but it was doing something interesting to my blood sugar levels. My body was starting to hum.

What to do?

First, I needed to get into my apartment. There was nothing stopping me from going in, but I wanted every dead thing out, except my cat. Then I was going to figure out why my place was full of ghosts and fix it.

There were two confections left. A cornucopia horn filled with pastry cream and dipped in nuts, and some kind of tart. I wanted to eat them both but I wanted the ghosts gone more. Which was a testament to how much sugar was already coursing around my body.

I marched into my apartment holding the box.

"Hey!" I said. "Listen up. You've got thirty seconds to get out or I'm calling an exorcist."

"She always threatens to do that," Yiorgos Dakis said. "Do not listen to her. Stand your ground."

"No—no standing your ground," I said. "This isn't your ground. It's my ground."

"Technically it is a second-floor apartment and therefore not on the ground," one of the ghosts said. He was vaguely familiar but I couldn't pin a name to him. From his 1960s outfit I guessed he was someone who'd died years ago. Didn't matter. He had to go with the rest of them.

"I have zero tolerance for pedants and other smartasses, unless they're my niece and nephew," I told him. "Now get out."

"No. We know you can see us. We know you can hear us, too."

"Spoiler alert: lots of people can see you," I lied. "We just ignore you because you're annoying."

"That is very mean," someone said.

"You're dead," I said. "You're ghosts. Now go do what ghosts are supposed to do, and do it far away from here."

"Haunt things?" someone asked.

"Go toward the light," I explained. "Head on up to the Afterlife. It's fun. They have games."

"How would you know?"

"Ghosts tell me things," I said. "Shoo now. Go on."

Another spirit shuffled forward. I recognized her as one of my sister's former neighbors. "We are not going anywhere. We have problems, and we heard you are the woman who can solve them."

Oh brother. This wasn't happening. This—*this*—was exactly why I didn't waltz around, flaunting my ability to see and hear dead people.

"Someone stole my chicken when I was still alive," she went on. "It was that *vromoskelo*, Yiannis Yiannopoulous."

"It was your daughter-in-law," I said. "She killed it, cooked it, and you ate it at her house one Sunday, after church."

"Really?"

"Really."

She eyed me suspiciously. "How do you know?"

"People tell me things."

She thought about it a moment. Then she vanished with a barely audible *pop*. Gone toward the light permanently, I hoped.

Another spirit waved his arm. I pointed to him.

"I cannot rest until I realize my dream of singing in Eurovision," he said.

"Yeah, that's never going to happen," I said.

"Then I will stay here."

Think, Allie. Solve the problem.

"Go sing down at the waterfront. Even at this time of year we get a few tourists. Maybe one of them will be able to see and hear you. Do you have a song prepared?"

He puffed up his chest. "My own composition. Do you want to hear it?"

"I really don't."

"It is called *My Goat, My Love, My Boat*."

I was sure I'd read it during my Dr. Seuss days. But I didn't say that. Dead or not, I didn't want to crush his dreams, I just wanted him to leave.

The other ghosts groaned. None of them fancied being an audience. Which made all of us.

"Fine," I said. "Sing your song."

"Will you judge me?"

"Do you want me to?"

"Of course."

My jaw clenched. My teeth ground together. "Okay. But then you have to go."

He sang--if I could call it that. Mostly I was glad no living person besides me could hear him, otherwise they'd report me for strangling cats. The style was *Rembetika*, a form of Greek folk music. At the best of times it made me want to claw out my eardrums. This was not the best of times. The goat sailed away with his woman and his boat, leaving him to mourn them all, especially the boat.

When he was done, I gave him a ten out of ten. He took a bow and disappeared.

"Who's next?" I said, resigned to my fate. If this was what it took to get rid of them all, I'd suffer through it. After this, though, Dead Cat and I would have to figure out some kind of plan so he could come and go as he pleased, while limiting the comings and goings of other spirits—especially the comings.

One at a time I worked through their problems. Most were satisfied with my simple fixes. I knew stuff, rocked at finding things, and between the two skillsets I managed to send a bunch of ghosts packing.

Two hours later, I was down to an empty cake box and a handful of dead folks, all of whom had bigger problems than I was equipped to handle.

"I want to know who murdered me," Konstantinos Grivas said.

"Detective Samaras is still working on that," I said.

Someone knocked on the door. Great. Perfect. Just what I needed. A half dozen ghosts yapping in my ear, demanding attention, while I had to fake being a normal, functioning human being.

The peephole said Lydia was on the other side. I opened the door. She waddled right in and plopped down on the couch.

"*Po-po*, my feet hurt," she said.

"Must be the high heels," I said. But she wasn't wearing high heels. She was in a pair of old slippers I recognized as Kyria Olga's. Her larger feet hung out the back. The cardigan was her grandmother's, too.

"New wardrobe?" I asked her.

She sidestepped the question. "Where did the *nanos* go? He annoys me. He is almost like a real person. A bantam rooster will never be a proper rooster."

It was one thing for me to mock Jimmy—we had a mutual thing going—but from Lydia it was just cruel.

"You hurt his feelings. He likes you, you know. You haven't noticed because he's always hiding in bushes, stalking you. But maybe try to be kind."

She picked up the pink jar on the coffee table, inspected it closely before setting it back down. "What is that?"

"I keep the tears of my enemies in there."

She looked at me.

"Was there something you wanted?" I asked.

"No." She picked up the remote, turned on the TV, began flicking through the channels. Not that we had many here on the island. During the day they showed Greek soaps. At night it was a combination of movies and comedies, Greek and English-language with subtitles.

"I'm kind of busy right now."

"You do not look busy," she said.

My Spidey senses tingled. Something was up, and that something was Lydia. I crouched down beside her, laid my palm on her forehead. Her face was hot enough to fry eggs and maybe a couple of pancakes.

"I think you need an aspirin," I said. "You're running a fever and you're wearing your grandmother's clothes."

The ghosts were interested in her. Too interested. They milled around her.

"*Po-po*, that one has problems," one of the dead women said. I didn't know her name. She was from before my time. All I knew about her was that she thought she'd been murdered. Maybe she had been, and I'd be able to find out more just as soon as I dealt with the immediate Lydia problem. "What you need is rubbing alcohol. Take off her *pandofles* and rub it on her feet."

"I'm not rubbing her anything," I said in a low voice.

Lydia looked at me. "Who are you talking to?"

"Myself."

She got up and wandered into my kitchen. I watched her rifle through the fridge. She unwrapped the kaseri and sniffed. "Kaseri? I have not had this in years. Too expensive."

"Greece's second most common cheese? Really?"

She held up the mortadella. "What is this?"

"Mortadella."

"Not enough fat. Not like the old days."

"Did you come here to criticize my cold cuts?"

She ignored me while she hacked a huge chunk of bread off the day-old loaf. Mortadella went on top, followed by a slab of kaseri. With a satisfied groan, she bit into one end and chewed.

"Starve a cold, feed a fever. Or is it the other way around?" I asked nobody in particular.

While she ate, I fired up my computer and searched a database for information about the woman who suspected she'd been murdered. Like Panos Grekos, the island's previous coroners all took meticulous notes. The woman had tripped on a chicken and fell on her own knitting needle. It shot up her nose, into her brain and killed her instantly. Witnesses all reported the same story.

"I do not believe it," she said. "A knitting needle?"

"That's what the coroner and witnesses said."

"I cannot knit."

"Yes, because you're dead."

"No—I could not knit when I was alive. My mother cried and cried when she realized I was as competent with knitting needles as a donkey. She said I would never find a husband. But I found a man with a wool allergy and he did not mind that I could not knit."

I eyed the kitchen. Lydia had finished her meal and was working on an encore snack of more kaseri—this time without bread or meat.

"What can you tell me about the witnesses?" I asked. I turned the screen so she could read their names.

She squinted. "I cannot read."

Squinting definitely wasn't going to help her, in that case. "You never learned?"

"In those days, if girls went to school they dropped out

after *dimitiko*, if not sooner. My parents pulled me out in the second grade after I mastered coloring between the lines."

Dimitiko. Elementary school.

"I can read the names for you."

I read the witness list to her and she shook her head. "None of them would kill me."

"True crime documentaries would beg to differ. Half the time, murders start with those who say they love you."

"My family did not love me. They were afraid, like a family should be. They trembled when I yelled."

Lovely. "So somebody probably did kill you to shut you up?"

"That is what I am saying."

Lydia stuck her head out. "More cheese."

"I don't have any more cheese."

"Where do I get more?"

"Your place?"

"My refrigerator is empty except for wine."

"The More Super Market or the Super Super Market?"

She pulled the cardigan around her body. "I will go there."

"Wait—what? You're running a fever. Probably you've got the flu, and it's freezing out there."

"I can withstand the cold. I have this …" she picked at a speck of lint "…cardigan."

I couldn't let her go. Not on her own, and preferably not at all.

"I'll go," I said.

"You will go to get more kaseri?"

"I'll go, but on one condition?"

"Name this … condition."

"Go back to bed." Probably I should clarify. "Your bed."

"You mean the bed across the hallway."

"Yes."

She thought about it for a moment. "Okay. Bring as much kaseri as you can carry."

"I'm not sure I can afford that much cheese."

She dug in her pocket and presented me with a single euro. "As much as you can buy with this."

My eye twitched.

I waited until she let herself into her apartment and shut the door behind her. Then I trotted downstairs to my bicycle. The world was losing its mind. Or maybe I was. Either way, things weren't right. I'd get Lydia her cheese, but then I was calling a doctor. On Merope you can still get a house call if necessary. Like all Greek healthcare, it was free, but it didn't hurt if you threw in a little envelope of cash for the doctor's trouble.

A car pulled up beside me. Leo. He rolled down the window.

"Where are you going, and why?"

I told him about Lydia, then I asked him what he knew about old murders.

"How old?"

"Say, a hundred years."

"That is old."

"Any idea where I can get information?"

"Merope has records going all the way back to the island's first inhabitants. Back then it was mostly accusations in picture form. I poked through them once. There are a lot of obscene hand gestures."

"Can I see the records?"

"I want something in return."

"Is it sex?"

"I want you to go home and rest like you're supposed to."

"So it's not sex?"

"Not tonight."

Good thing he didn't know I'd zipped off to England for the morning and almost wound up as mincemeat under a construction worker's boot.

"But Lydia's cheese."

He looked at me. I looked back. We were at an impasse. In the cold. With the wind whipping around us.

Leo caved first. He got out and stuck my bicycle in the trunk and drove me to the More Super Market. I ordered half a wheel. Was it enough?

"Make it a whole," I told the deli guy.

Leo's eyebrows rose. "That's a lot of cheese."

"Is it though? I can eat a lot of kaseri in one sitting. And besides, Lydia told me to buy as much as I could carry."

"Is she paying for this?"

I handed him the euro she'd given me. He raised an eyebrow.

"Maybe thirty years ago," he said.

"She's sick. I think it's the flu."

When we got to the counter, he pulled out his wallet and handed Stephanie a short stack of cash.

Mentally, I objected to him paying. Stephanie could barely cope with credit and debit cards. Us arguing over who was going to pay would break her brain. And it would definitely get her talking. Before long—I'd give it until morning, seeing as it was getting late—the whole island would know. Wouldn't be long before they'd consider us broken up, after a vicious, physical fight. So to keep us out of the mouths of local gossips, I kept quiet. I'd repay him later.

Leo carried the cheese back to his car, then he drove us home. When we got upstairs, I knocked while Leo carried cheese.

Lydia yanked the door open, snatched the cheese out of his arms, slammed the door in his face. Leo looked puzzled.

"What's wrong with her?"

"Bitch flu."

He laughed. I didn't.

"She called Jimmy a *nanos*."

Leo winced. "Ouch."

"He was hurt, I could tell. It's not like Lydia to be mean."

He frowned. "She was wearing a lot of clothes for Lydia."

Something was bothering me—something beyond the myriad other things. I couldn't put my finger on it yet, but it was there, simmering below the surface. Every time I tried to grab it, it swam away. Why I was using a fish analogy I didn't know.

My phone rang. Christos Fekkas was on the other end.

"Can we talk?"

"We're talking right now."

"I mean in person."

"Sure. Is it Yiayia?" A band tightened around my head. "Did someone dig her up again? We only just put her back."

"It would be better if you come to the cemetery."

Nothing good ever came from someone inviting you to a cemetery, but this was Christos Fekkas. We trusted him with the dead, and for the most part he cared for them without incident and only a tiny bit of weirdness.

"When?" I asked him.

"In the morning?"

I relaxed. I wouldn't have to wait until Leo left before sneaking out. As far as I was concerned, when the sun came up his protective order would evaporate. Then I'd be my own woman again, free to roam. Or something like that.

We agreed on a time. I ended the call.

Leo gave me an expectant look.

"Christos Fekkas," I said. "He wants to talk."

"Everything okay?"

"Probably he heard about my trip to the hospital and wants to talk me into buying my own plot."

"Don't joke about that. I just found you. I don't know what I'd do if I lost you."

"Just found me? We met in high school."

He grinned. "You know what I mean. Tomorrow?"

"Tomorrow," I said.

He kissed me lightly. "Good. Tonight I expect you to sleep."

"Bossy."

"Only when it comes to your health and safety."

"Only then?"

My meaning was clear.

He grinned. "You'll find out soon."

I swallowed. I wanted to find out now, maybe try out his handcuffs while we were at it. Handcuffs seemed like they were a lot of fun when someone like Leo had the key.

CHAPTER SEVENTEEN

The DOCTOR ARRIVED with his leather bag and a persistent hearing problem. Doctor Roros was a tall, thin man with a face that was half nose and one quarter thick, black mustache. His pants sat too high, revealing several centimeters of white sock between his hem and polished shoes. He was wearing a Nehru jacket that he'd owned since the 1980s.

"She likes cheese," he said. "Does she normally like cheese?"

Lydia was sitting on the couch in front of the television, knocking back kaseri cheese like it was her calling in life. Maybe it was. Good cheese is pretty persuasive. Some nights it hollers at me, especially if it's feta tucked inside a *tiropita* or *spanakopita*.

"I don't know. Doesn't everyone?"

"My mother did not like cheese, and look at her now."

His mother had passed years ago. "Isn't she ..." I tried to find a tactful way to say *dead* "... no longer with us?"

"Possibly because she did not like cheese. How do you feel?" he asked Lydia.

"Like the cow next to you didn't buy enough cheese."

He looked around for a cow.

"She means me," I said. "I'm the cow."

"Her grandmother was such a nice woman." He pulled the cheese out of her hand and stuck a thermometer in her mouth. When he inspected it, he frowned.

"This is a problem."

"Fever?"

"Your friend is cooking from the inside out." He called for an ambulance.

"I'm not going anywhere without my cheese," Lydia said.

"You can take your cheese," I said.

She hugged the wheel and the chunk she'd already cut out of it.

The ambulance arrived.

"She's cooking from the inside out," I told the paramedics.

"She looks fine, except for the clothes and the cheese."

Looks were deceiving, and I should know. My fiancé seemed perfectly fine until he dropped dead in the Super Super Market from a heart problem. I didn't want Lydia to die. When she wasn't being weird and devouring cheese, she was an okay person. A bit prickly and distant, but the potential was there. Did she have a will? She owned the whole building, except for my apartment, which her grand-mother had left to me. If she died, who would get the building? I knew her relatives. I wished I didn't.

"I'm going with her," I told the paramedics and climbed in. I watched as they hooked Lydia up to IV fluids and tried to wrestle the cheese away.

"Don't mess with the cheese," I said.

"Can we at least have the cardigan?"

I looked at Lydia. She nodded.

"You can have the cardigan," I said.

They performed an elaborate and rehearsed ballet to remove the cardigan while Lydia clung to her cheese.

"Is there some disease where people eat cheese?" I asked them. They were in the medical field. They knew things. Paramedics got to see all the weird stuff, especially on Merope during tourist season.

"Who doesn't eat cheese?" they said.

"Like this?" I said, gesturing at Lydia, who was biting straight into the cheese wheel. None of us wanted to give her a knife.

"I've never seen anybody eat cheese like that," the paramedic admitted, "except my wife when she was pregnant."

Maybe she was pregnant but I didn't think so. Lydia struck me as the sensible kind of person who took things like protection and birth control seriously.

Five minutes later they were wheeling Lydia into the emergency room. The place was quiet. Merope didn't get a lot of emergencies outside of the summer months, when tourists came here to do dumb things they'd never do at home. The nurses were hanging out, gossiping and playing games on their phones.

They wheeled Lydia away and promised me they wouldn't try to separate her from her cheese.

I flopped down in a chair and closed my eyes.

Before I knew it, an hour had passed and one of the nurses was shaking me awake.

"You can go home. We're keeping your friend … and her cheese."

"Can I see her?"

She said I could and gave me Lydia's room number.

Lydia was propped up in bed, gnawing on the big

wheel of cheese. She had an IV in each hand and she was covered in cooling blankets.

"Don't just stand there," she said when she saw me. "Go get more cheese."

"No can do. The shops are closed."

"My mother's *mouni*," she said.

———

Twenty minutes later, I was home. The ghosts perked up. I held up one finger, on account of how holding up a whole hand would be an insult.

"Anyone speaks and I'm calling the Ghostbusters. Right now I need sleep. If you don't let me sleep, I won't help you. I'll do the opposite of that. Are we clear?"

They got the message but they weren't happy about it. I didn't care. I needed sleep, and I needed it now. Last night's adventures, today's shenanigans, and Lydia's cheese obsession had drained me dry.

As I settled down in bed and hoisted the covers up to my neck, a familiar weight plonked itself on my chest. Dead Cat was home.

Something cold tickled my face.

"No, kitty. This is my sleepy time."

He meowed. A tiny sound for a cat the size of a small bus.

"No, kitty, kitty."

He jumped off the bed and yowled. Dead Cat never yowled. Mostly he ghost-peed on people he didn't like.

I sat up. He turned around and sauntered out the door, glancing over one misty shoulder.

Fine. *Fine.* I'd get up, but just this once.

I followed him to the living room. The ghosts leaped to

their feet. I held up the warning finger. They sat back down.

"What is it?" I asked my cat.

He jumped up on the coffee table, sashayed back and forth, his tail flicking.

What was he trying to tell me?

I didn't speak cat. I'd never had a pet before Dead Cat. And he didn't require all the usual feline accessories. No litter box. No food bowl. No water fountain to keep water constantly fresh. He used anything he wanted as a scratching post and never left a mark.

"Going back to bed now," I said.

CHAPTER EIGHTEEN

"Whatever has the most caffeine and sugar, give me that," I told the barista at Merope's Best.

Her expression of ennui morphed into concern. "We don't normally give that to people over forty."

"I'm thirty-one."

She wasn't convinced. "Are you sure?"

"I had a busy day yesterday. It's harder to recover once you hit thirty."

"That's probably it."

Five minutes later and several whispers with her co-workers later, she presented me with a paper cup as tall as my head.

"Yowza," I said after the first sip. The caffeine and sugar rocketed straight to my bloodstream. My heart began to bounce off my ribs. It mistook them for a trampoline. I took another sip. Colors brightened. A marathon sounded like an acceptable idea. Should I repaint my apartment? My eye twitched. No—my eye wasn't moving. The rest of me was jittering around it.

"We call it the *Malakismeni*," she said. "It's off-menu."

Malakismeni. One of those words without a direct translation. Crazy, in a completely messed up and masturbatory way.

I gave her ten euros and she crossed herself.

"If you end up in the emergency room, we know nothing," she said.

Christos Fekkas was waiting for me at the cemetery. He paled when he saw my cup.

"Malakismeni?"

"You know it?"

"Never tried it, but they did." He pointed to three gravestones.

Yikes. "Should I buy a plot now?"

"Wait until after Christmas when there's a two-for-one sale."

Was he joking? I couldn't tell. "So what couldn't you tell me over the phone?"

He hesitated. That couldn't be good.

"I need to show you something."

"What is it?"

With the toe of his boot, he nudged a wandering pebble off the path and back with its brethren. "I looked in your grandmother's coffin before it was time to rebury her. It sounds weird but it's not. I always check."

That made sense. "It's like when you buy shoes and the cashier opens the box and they check that the shoes are the same size and the same brand as what's on the box."

"They do that?"

Not on Merope they didn't. If you wanted your shoes to match you had to check them yourself. "In America they do. So what happened when you checked Yiayia's casket?"

"She wasn't in there."

My lungs deflated. Was it panic or the coffee? "Empty?"

"No. Someone was in there. But it wasn't her."

"Could you even tell? She's been dead a while. Things are bound to be goopy."

"The body was new."

"New?"

He glanced around furtively, as if the dead had ears they were using. Mind you, on Merope it was possible even corpses passed on gossip. If it could happen anywhere it was here.

"It was Maria Griva."

Malakismeni shot down the wrong hole. I spluttered. Christos patted me on the back.

"Maria Griva is dead?"

"That is what I am saying."

"Did you call the police?"

"Not yet. I was concerned they might think I messed up. I never mix up bodies or burial plots. Everyone rests where they're supposed to."

"So where is my grandmother?"

He shrugged. "Not in her coffin."

"And she was before, right?"

"Yes. I checked before she went into the ground the first time."

That familiar steel band settled around my forehead and gave it a big bear hug. None of my problems were going away. They were snowballing, picking up complications and other random debris for the downhill ride.

I took a swig of the supercharged coffee—without choking, this time. My blood pressure jumped to new heights. Christos was waiting for me to make decisions here. Why me? Dead people were his thing. I only did ghosts.

Speaking of ghosts, I performed a quick visual inspection of the cemetery. Maria Griva wasn't hanging around her body, and if she'd been murdered she hadn't come to find me. Which was nice. I didn't need more ghosts showing up, expecting me to resolve their life stories. As soon as I found out who'd spilled their guts about my abilities, I was going to stomp my foot, make vague threats, and maybe raise my voice. Also, I'd do a lot of sarcasm. Play to your strengths, I say.

"Everyone on Merope knows you're dedicated to your work," I said, doing my best to reassure the concerned caretaker. "Don't worry."

I called Leo.

"Situation at the cemetery," I said.

"What kind of situation?"

"Another dead body."

There was a pause. Then: "At a cemetery?"

His smartassery made me smile. Or maybe it was the *Malakismeni* I was sucking down, living up to its name. "This one is in my grandmother's coffin. And before you ask, it's not Yiayia. And before you ask, I don't know where she is."

"I'm not going to ask how you know all this."

"Probably for the best."

He promised he was on his way, and five minutes later he turned in to the parking lot with Pappas behind him. Both policemen joined me at Yiayia's open grave. They stared down into the hole.

"So do we know who's in coffin now?" Leo asked.

"Maria Griva," I said.

"How do you know?"

"Christos checks all the coffins before they go in. It's like checking shoes."

"Do I want to know?"

"Probably best if you don't."

"This is a problem," he said, looking down at the sooty

casket. "Maria Griva was the primary suspect for her husband's murder."

"It's always the wife," I said.

He looked at me.

"That's what true crime documentaries say."

Pappas paled. "Do I have to look at the body?"

"First we need to bring it up," Leo told him.

"I'm going to throw up now, in advance," Pappas said. "That way I won't embarrass myself. Is there a bathroom around here?"

He went inside to look for a bathroom or something that passed as one. I was pretty sure the bathroom was whatever or wherever you made it in the cemetery.

Leo went off to talk to Christos Fekkas about raising the dead.

Which left me at a loose end.

Konstantinos Grivas was dead, and now his wife had passed, too. Yiayia's body was missing. What linked them together, besides death, was their circle of friends.

While the police were busy with their police work, I went to look for answers.

––––––––

Greece is a country of universal healthcare, and Merope is an island with mostly empty hospital beds during the cold months and a vested interest in taking precautions when it comes to its senior population. Yiayia's friends had all suffered from a variety of maladies when they were hauled in, from smoke inhalation to broken bones. Plus they were in a legal gray area after stealing Yiayia's coffin and body. The police were in the process of deciding what to do with them. So the hospital was keeping them for the time being.

Which made my job easier. One location; all the suspects.

I picked the weakest of the bunch, the most likely to blab. But Vicki Niki was asleep when I peeped in. So I went to the ringleader, Kyria Eugenia herself.

She was propped up in bed, stabbing fabric stretched over an embroidery hoop. Her head was three quarters bandage, on account of how she'd stuck her head in fire. I tilted my blissfully not-burnt head to read the words.

"The short woman *hestika*," she said.

The short woman crapped herself. A popular Greek saying that meant "Big deal, so what?"

I planted myself in one of the faux leather chairs that farted if you sat too quickly. "You said your ritual worked."

"It worked."

"So, Yiayia is back? Risen from the dead like Lazarus or Jesus?"

Deep down—just below the liter of coffee in my belly —I didn't believe some woo-woo ritual or spell could bring anyone back. There were limits to the ways my mind stretched. It stuck to the possible and probable. Despite seeing ghosts, traveling through portals, and buying cake from a shop not everyone could see, and that existed in every time and place, I longed to be a skeptic. Skepticism was easy. Believe nothing. Demand proof. Twitch a lot.

"If she is not yet, she will be. The timing is not precise." She didn't sound convinced.

"Doesn't sound to me like you were adequately prepared."

The needle quit stabbing. "Why are you speaking Chinese? Speak Greek so I can understand you."

I leaned in the doorway, arms folded. If I sat I'd be lower. I wanted to keep the upper hand, even if it was just physically and in my own head.

"Tell me what was supposed to happen, provided the ritual worked perfectly."

"It did work perfectly."

"Tell me anyway. Pretend I'm a *vlakas*."

"For that I do not have to pretend."

"Be nice or I'll tell the nurse you want an enema."

"I could use a good *kaka*."

This old biddy had a steel spine. No wonder she and Yiayia were frenemies their whole lives. "Just tell me how it was supposed to work."

"The ritual was to bring back your grandmother's soul and place it in Vicki Niki's body."

"That's it?"

"What else did you expect?"

"More details, for one. What happens to Vicky Niki's soul? And what about Yiayia's body?"

"What about her body? It goes on decaying, of use to nobody except worms."

"You couldn't bring Yiayia back and put her back in her own body?"

She made a face. Or that was just her regular face. Hard to say with all the bandages. "I do not know anything about reanimating dead flesh, only placing a soul in a living body."

"I checked on Vicki Niki. She's not my grandmother. Not even a little bit. Still."

"She has to be. The ritual worked perfectly, except for the part where you showed up and stuck your nose into our business."

"Hypothetically speaking, if Yiayia didn't end up in her intended new living space, where might she have gone?"

"I suppose she could be in a different body."

"And what happens to the soul already in that body? You didn't answer that. Does it scoot over and make room?

Vacate completely and find another living space? Battle for supremacy? Challenge the new soul to a dance-off?"

"I do not know."

"Seems to me like these are things you should know before you start waving a magic book around. Yiayia's body is gone. It's not in its coffin. Know anything about that?"

She quit stabbing the white cotton like it was a mortal enemy.

"What are you saying?"

"Someone switched Yiayia out with Maria Griva."

Her head jerked up. "Maria is dead?"

"Deader than *Mega Alexandros*."

Mega Alexandros was Alexander the Great. The Greek language regularly swaps words around. Around these parts, the king was known as Big Alexander.

She cast aside the needlepoint and grabbed the doodad that made bits of the bed go up and down. She jabbed the red button. A nurse stuck her head into the room.

"This *tsigana* is trying to steal my money," Kyria Eugenia said.

The nurse looked at me. I wasn't Romany and she knew it. Merope didn't have Romany people.

"You should probably go," the nurse told me.

"But—"

"*Tsigana!*" Kyria Eugenia yelled. "*Stinky, curse-ridden tsigana! You are all the same, except you dress a little better!*"

Nobody did bigotry and racism like old Greeks.

"I have questions—"

"Go before she starts insulting my mother for buying the last chicken in the meat shop fifteen years ago," the nurse said. "And don't forget to buy cheese for your friend. She has already eaten most of our kaseri supply. Who eats that much cheese besides the French?"

Lydia. I'd forgotten about her cheese, what with needing to sleep and have a life.

I slipped out of the room and went downstairs to rustle up another coffee. This one didn't have the *Malakismeni's* kick. But it did have a shot of chocolate, so it was practically dessert. I bought a *koulouri*—a skinny, loop of soft pretzel, dipped in sesame seeds—for the fiber and the buffer, and consumed them both while I contemplated what I knew.

My job was easier when it was finding objects.

Also, it was my job.

Apart from the unrelated Angela angle, which was me searching for a friend, nobody was hiring me to untangle this … whatever this was Yiayia had got herself mixed up in. I didn't even know what to call it. A death pact? A life pact? I was going nuts for the low, low price of free.

If it really was a life pact, why come back in an old body that didn't have a lot of tread left on the tires? If it were me—and it never would be, because *eww* and also *weird*—I'd come back in a young body, one that didn't have sore feet and failing eyesight.

I picked a sesame seed out from between my teeth.

What was I missing? For someone who finds things, I wasn't finding diddly.

I went back to check on Vicky Niki, the intended vessel for Yiayia's soul. She was awake now and hadn't received the memo that I was a thieving Romany, out to steal her money. She and her sagging bouffant didn't look perturbed when I told her Maria Griva was dead and currently hiding out in my grandmother's coffin.

"That happens a lot when you get to my age," she said. "Except usually people get their own coffins. Greece's economy is a disaster." Flecks of spit hit the floor. "Turks."

I was pretty sure Greece's money woes were the result

of tax dodging, greedy, incompetent politicians, and a variety of other maladies that had nothing to do with Turks, for a change, but I didn't say that.

"Are you my grandmother yet?"

"No, I am still myself." Her face fell. "I was hoping to have some fun before I die, even with these sore feet."

"You can still have fun."

"Not with this personality."

A stray thought wiggled to the surface. "Maria Griva was one of Yiayia's best friends. Why wasn't she part of this pact or whatever it was? Now that I think about it, I didn't see her when you were all stealing Yiayia's coffin."

She made a face. "She was supposed to be there."

"So she knew about it?"

"Of course. We all did. The plan was set into motion long before your grandmother died."

And yet Maria Griva had tried to hire me because her husband was consorting with the devil. Why involve me when she was privy to the whole plan?

The answer, when it came, was more of a peep than a flash. Suddenly I really needed to talk to her dead husband.

"Vinegar," I said. "That really helps if you rub it on your feet."

"That is what they keep telling me," she said, "but it never works. I think I just enjoy complaining."

———

I peddled back home and all but threw my bicycle against the wall in my haste to get back to my apartment. When I got there, the remaining ghosts leaped to attention. You'd think the dead would be more relaxed.

"Kyrios Grivas?" I said to the dead woman's also-dead

husband. "Your wife knew about the plan to bring Yiayia back, yes?"

He hung his head. His expression was pure guilt. "She knew but she did not approve."

"Why?"

"She said it was the work of the devil."

I moved on. "Who were you trying to contact with that spirit board the police found with you? Your wife mentioned the devil."

"The devil. Ha. I was trying to contact your grandmother, and my wife knew it."

"Why try to contact her if you were all about to bring her back?"

"The man in the black clothes said I could talk to her through the board. He gave me the board and told me to make sure your grandmother truly wanted to come back. People often change their minds after they pass, he said."

That got my attention. "Man in black?"

"A stranger. A *xenos*. I never saw him on Merope before."

A foreigner? That sounded like *the* Man in Black. "Long coat? Dark hair. Moody visage?"

He waggled his head enthusiastically. "Did he give you a spirit board, too?"

"He gave me a salt shaker."

"I hope it worked better than the spirit board."

"It salts things."

His face fell. "My spirit board must have been a dud."

"Can you think of any reason your wife wouldn't have wanted my grandmother to come back? Besides the devil thing."

Yiorgos Dakis laughed. "Why do you think?"

Konstantinos Grivas elbowed him. It went straight through. "*Skasmos!*"

"You may as well tell me," I said. "One way or another I'll find out."

"She is good at finding things," Yiorgos Dakis said. He made a circle with his fingers and poked it. "That is what he was doing with your grandmother. We all were."

My eye twitched. This case needed to be over before I lost a lifetime of lunches.

"Not all of us," Konstantinos Grivas said. "Not me."

"So you weren't sleeping with her?" I said. "That's a relief."

"But my wife was. I caught them playing hide the *loukaniko* with a real *loukaniko*."

Loukaniko is a sausage. It's spiced with things like orange peel and fennel.

"Your wife was sleeping with Yiayia? Kyria Maria? I'm so confused." I fell onto the couch, closed my eyes. "I need more sleep, less coffee, and fewer ghosts."

"We are not going anywhere until you help us," the chorus of dead people said.

"Yes, I've got that," I snapped.

Someone knocked on the door. It was Jimmy. Against my better judgment I opened the door. He took it as an invitation.

"I was worried about your mental health. I heard you talking to yourself," he said.

"Worry more about people who don't," I said. "They're the real weirdoes."

He made a face like something was on his mind. "Lydia is in the hospital. I was thinking I should go see her, maybe take her flowers."

"Kaseri."

"Cheese? Really?"

"Really," I said.

"I guess I could pick up a piece of cheese if she likes cheese."

"No—more cheese."

"How much cheese are we talking about?"

"How much can you carry?"

"Probably a lot on account of how I've been plowing fields."

I didn't want to picture Jimmy plowing anything, not even a field. "That was one day."

"There were a lot of retakes."

Jimmy left with his shopping list of one item. Lydia's cheese fever was another weird event on a whole pile of weird events right now. But seeing as how she was in the hospital with the best of Merope's medical professionals taking care of her, she wasn't my top priority.

"So let me get this straight," I said, trying to make sense of this bizarre king rat. "My grandmother was having affairs with everyone, including your wife?"

"Yes," Konstantinos Grivas said.

"But not you."

"No."

"Why not?"

"Because I love my wife. There was never another woman for me. I did not want your grandmother to come back. With her gone, my wife was my wife."

"Until you were murdered."

"That was a problem."

I realized I'd been negligent in duties that weren't normally my duties. Konstantinos Grivas's wife was dead and nobody had notified him. The police couldn't soften the bad news for him because, as far as they were concerned, he didn't exist anymore. Which meant it was up to me.

"Kyrios Grivas, your wife has passed," I said. "I'm so

sorry." I almost tacked on "*na zeiseis*," which means, "may you live". But I figured since he was already dead, the standard Greek etiquette would be pointless and insensitive.

He blinked. A lot. The spirit keeps a lot of the flesh's old habits. They never truly die. I told him what I knew, which wasn't much.

"I know," he said. "I love her. Being a ghost meant I could follow her around without her knowing."

Was that sweet or creepy? The jury was still out.

"Do you have any idea who might have killed her and hidden her in my grandmother's casket?"

"Yes," he said.

I waited.

"She did it herself, and I watched her."

"Why?"

"She was sick, and she wanted to go."

The woman hadn't seemed sick. The beating she gave Leo with her footwear was serious.

"So she drank a cup of hemlock and jumped into Yiayia's coffin?"

"My wife saw an opportunity and took it. She climbed into your grandmother's coffin and waited for the fire to get her."

"But the lack of oxygen or the smoke got to her first?"

"Yes."

"What about Yiayia's remains?"

"I did not see any remains."

"The casket was empty?"

"Empty, and cleaner than a new pair of Greek underpants."

A clean, empty casket meant one thing: Yiayia's final resting place was a lie.

The harder I tried to loosen the knots, the tighter the rope got. One person would know if my grandmother had ever taken that slow, downward elevator. But what if Christos Fekkas was involved? People talked about him, but the talk was positive. He did a good job taking care of the island's dead, even if he did prefer hanging out in the cemetery to drinking coffee at the *kafeneios* and fishing. No one had ever caught him canoodling with one of his charges. The island did have a closeted necrophiliac, but that person's tastes leaned toward poultry. And it wasn't Christos Fekkas.

I had to see Christos. I also wanted Konstantinos Grivas to stay close in case I had more questions.

"Come to the cemetery?" I said.

He hesitated. "I do not know …"

"It's just a graveyard."

"But there are ghosts there," he said like he wasn't one himself.

"Have you looked in a mirror lately?"

"Yes, but I am not there."

"That's right. You're a ghost. Therefore there's nothing to be afraid of at the cemetery. For what it's worth, I've never seen a single ghost there."

"Maybe that is because you were not looking."

The remaining ghosts in my apartment didn't look impressed. They wanted me to get on with the jobs they weren't paying me for. And was it my imagination or were there a few more now? I had to do something—and soon.

"Please," I said.

Grivas made a face. "I suppose I could, since you are working on my murder."

His murder was Leo's jurisdiction but I didn't remind him. Right now I maybe needed him.

"Meet you there," I said.

"Why? I am coming with you."

CHAPTER NINETEEN

I SEE DEAD PEOPLE.

I also see through dead people.

Merope was Grivas-colored as I peddled through the village and out to the cemetery. Unconstrained by the limits of a human body—at least one that had never tried yoga—Konstantinos Grivas folded himself in to my bicycle's basket, his limbs dangling dangerously over the edges. Every time his foot touched the wheel, he yelped.

"Could you stop that?" I said.

"Why are you denying a dead man the chance to feel alive?"

I wanted to roll my eyes but I also needed to focus on the dirt road, which had seen smoother times.

When the road turned into the cemetery's driveway, Grivas farted and vanished. So much for sticking around to help me.

Christos Fekkas was in the shed, working on what appeared to be a map of the cemetery.

"Current and future plots," he explained when he saw

me. "How can I help you? Nobody else died in my ceme-tery, did they?"

I watched him carefully as I told him what I knew: that Yiayia had never taken that short elevator ride into Merope's dirt. If he lied, I liked to think I'd see it.

Guilt immediately smeared itself all over his face. "How did you know?"

"You wouldn't believe me if I told you. Let's just say I do. Where is my grandmother's body?"

"In the sea," he said simply and without hesitation. "I put her there myself. Rolled her right over the edge of the cliff, up by the old church."

Toula was going to flip, and not in a good way. "Why?"

"She paid me to do it. It doesn't look like it right now, I know, but I am an honorable man and those were her wishes."

"But why?"

"You would have to ask her."

As if I could do that. Not only was Yiayia dead, but she'd never once dropped by to give me wildly inappro-priate yet practical life advice.

The floor went wonky. Or maybe it was me. I found the nearest chair and waited for the world to stop spinning.

"There is something else you should know," Christos went on.

Of course there was. That was my life lately. "What?"

"Another person tried to pay me for her body, not long after she died, but I would not let him have her."

"Who?"

"That Englishman who died recently."

Roger Wilson. Warden of tiny ghost prisons. He'd trapped spirits in little jars, like the one on my coffee table, because ghosts were annoying. Like me, he could see them and got his kicks making them suffer. I got it. I did. Ghosts were a pain in the butt. But locking them up wasn't the way to go. All that did was create poltergeists when they finally got loose.

"That lunatic wanted Yiayia's body? Why?" It didn't make sense. Wilson's beef was with ghosts.

"He said your grandmother was annoying and he wanted to get rid of her forever."

In life, Yiayia was handful, that was true. But what was that to Roger Wilson?

I'd hit a roadblock. Roger Wilson was dead. He'd gobbled mass quantities of salt, and then a furious poltergeist finished him off. His ghost had come back to hassle me into solving his murder. In the end, he wound up sucked into a swirling hole that appeared in my ceiling. Apparently there was some cosmic authority out there that frowned on imprisoning the dead. Law enforcement turned out to be as inevitable as death and taxes.

"So you filled Yiayia's grave with an empty casket?"

"It was empty until someone put Maria Griva in there."

I told him what I knew. "Apparently she put in there herself. She was sick and she decided it was time to go."

"People," he said. "They are why I prefer the dead."

The inside of my mind resembled a mosh pit. There was only so much room and everything was thrashing around, battling to find a slot that made sense. "I don't suppose you have proof my grandmother asked you to pitch her body into the ocean after her death?"

"She put it in writing. I keep meticulous records. You never know when you'll need something. Like today."

Christos Fekkas wasn't lying. Not thirty seconds later, he presented me with a letter written in Yiayia's own handwriting. She'd left him specific orders. She wanted to be dumped in the sea, and when that happened she wanted to be wearing a yellow bikini. No black. She'd left instructions about her toy collection, too.

I winced. "Did you do all this?"

"She bought a bikini specifically for the occasion." He made a face. "It was small, and it had a string that went right up her—"

"I get the picture," I said. "And the … other stuff?"

"I had to break into her house, and I had to bring a truck. Your grandmother was a woman with a lot of toys. She kept them in a big trunk."

I knew the trunk. She'd told Toula and I never to look inside, otherwise we'd turn to salt. Since we'd heard all the Bible stories, and knew about Lot's wife, we pledged never to take any chances.

"And they are … where?"

"In the sea, with her body."

Great. So the sea around Merope was home to a trunk of dildos. All hell would break loose when the wood rotted and they started washing up on the beaches.

"I don't know what to say about any of this, so I'm going home now. Then I'm going to sleep. And hopefully when I wake up it'll be next year and my life will be normal again." I thought about it for a moment. "Normalish."

Christos wasn't done with me. "How did you know Maria Griva ended her own life?"

I thought about lying. But Christos Fekkas had fulfilled my grandmother's last wishes, right down to the bikini, and he'd answered my questions truthfully, as far as I could tell.

"Her husband told me," I said.

He nodded like that was the most reasonable thing in the world. "I figured."

———

Konstantinos Grivas reappeared with a *pop* as I rode out of the driveway. I swerved to avoid an olive tree.

"Rude," he said.

"Hey, you're the one who disappeared."

"Not you. I cannot enter the cemetery. Who tries to keep ghosts out of a cemetery?"

"Ghosts don't hang around cemeteries anyway," I said. "Why would they?"

My phone rang. Leo was on the other end.

"Panos says Konstantinos Grivas was stabbed during intercourse."

I passed on the message to the ghost in my wire basket.

"So that is why I died with no pants on," he said.

"Who were you with?" I asked him.

"My wife," he said. "It could not have been anyone else. Did I get to finish?"

I relayed the question to Leo.

"Do I want to know why you're asking?"

"I'm just the messenger," I said.

"I don't know and I don't want to know. Panos told me Maria Griva also had intercourse not long before someone put her into your grandmother's coffin."

"So you think she killed her husband?"

"She would never kill me!" Grivas said.

"How sure are you?" I asked him.

"Why would she? I was a good husband."

"A good husband who caught his wife boning my grandmother with an actual sausage," I said.

"Technically your grandmother was the one holding the sausage," he said.

"Everything about this conversation is disturbing," Leo said. "Are you saying Maria Griva was having an affair with your grandmother?"

"Be grateful you can only hear half of it. Probably I'm

scarred for life. Yiayia was sleeping with everyone," I said. "She was known for it. And I don't think it's out of the realm of possibility that Maria Griva killed her husband. I kind of want to kill him myself."

"You are as mean as your grandmother," Grivas told me. "They said you would be nicer."

"She probably stabbed him so he'd shut up," I told Leo.

"Murder suicide?" he said.

"Maybe. But the pieces don't feel like a perfect fit. Why kill her husband if she was going to end her own life anyway?"

"To avoid jail time?"

My head hurt. I needed to put this all in a spreadsheet. Once everything was laid out neatly in a grid I'd be able to look for patterns or fall asleep trying.

"I have to go," Leo said.

"Police work?"

"Lunch. Pappas wants to go to Crusty Dimitri's."

"What? On purpose?"

"I'm going with him to make sure he doesn't eat bugs. And just so you know, Eugenia Droulia checked herself out of the hospital."

"With those burns?"

"I'm just the messenger," he said with a grin, flinging my words back at me.

I left Leo to his hot garbage lunch and rode home. Lunch was on my mind as I rifled through my cupboards. Lydia had eaten all my cheese. There was no chance of a decent sandwich until I could be bothered going to the store.

"My wife loved cheese," Konstantinos Grivas said when I complained.

"Everybody loves cheese," I said.

"Not like she loved cheese. She always complained it was too expensive, so she would steal pieces from her friends' houses when they were not looking."

My couch was currently holding three ghost people and an annoyed Dead Cat, who was sprawled over the armrest. I shooed one of them away and sat next to my cat. He was staring at the table, his normally malevolent expression veering more toward perturbed.

Then I saw it. Or rather, didn't see it.

The pink jar was missing.

I crouched down. It wasn't under the couch, table, or anywhere else on the floor. I didn't have enough furniture to hide things well or for long.

"Did anyone see a pink jar?" I asked.

The ghosts glanced at each other.

"Maybe we saw something," one of them said. He was dressed like a goatherd from a bygone century. Probably because he was a goatherd from a bygone century.

I gave him a pretty good stink-eye. "Well?"

He stuck a finger in his ear, mushed it around. "The information is stuck. If you help me, could be it will come loose."

"Okay." I asked him his name and what he wanted.

"I was murdered. Find out who killed me and get revenge."

"I don't do revenge."

He sat down. "Then I do not know what happened to your jar."

My eye twitched. I fired up my computer, plugged his name into several databases. There he was. Someone had even turned his death into art.

"What is that?" he said, horrified.

"The art installation is called *Nature Takes its Revenge*.

Looks like you were eaten by your own goats while you were sleeping on the job."

"Goats do not eat people."

"They will if they start with your clothes and accidentally keep on going."

He faded to almost nothing. "Stick your jar up your *kolos*." Then he vanished. Wherever he was going, I hoped there were goats. Lots and lots of hungry goats.

"Anyone else want to be totally unhelpful?" I asked.

Everybody, it seemed. They all wanted something first. And because they were dead their timetables weren't exactly tight. They could wait forever.

But it didn't matter, because suddenly I realized where my jar had gone.

CHAPTER TWENTY

I RODE to the More Super Market and ordered kaseri. Not a whole wheel this time. Just a modest chunk that would last me a few days if I sliced it thin and put it on a sandwich like an American.

"What news?" I asked Stephanie Dolas.

"Kyria Eugenia was in here earlier, asking if I want a gangbang. I heard she is asking everyone."

Twitch. "A gangbang?"

"That is when a bunch of people get together and—"

"I know what it is," I said quickly before she could give me her definition. "This was Eugenia Droulia, yes?"

Stephanie indicated yes. "She looks like a mummy with those bandages wrapped around her head. Is it true you tried to burn off her hair?"

"What? No."

She shrugged. "That is what people are saying."

"Her burns are self-inflicted. Tell people that."

"Really?"

"Really. She jumped on a fire and hugged it tight."

"People might not believe that."

"Because it's true?"

She handed me my change. "Exactly."

———

I took my cheese with me to the hospital. Specifically, Lydia's room. She was propped up in bed without cheese, still wrapped in cooling blankets. The numbers on the machine constantly checking her vitals said her heart rate was high and her oxygen was low.

I sat in the chair, put my feet up on the bed. Unwrapped my cheese.

"What's your name?" I asked her.

"Are you going to share that cheese?"

"For the low, low price of telling me your name, you can have some."

Her tongue touched her bottom lip. "Lydia."

"What's your mother's name?"

"Cheese."

"Your mother's name."

"Cheese."

"You can't tell me, can you?"

"You promised you would share if I told you my name."

Jimmy walked in with cheese. A lot of cheese. He was rolling a wagon behind him filled with wheels of fresh kaseri.

"You brought cheese?" he said, eyeing the packet in my hand. "I was bringing the cheese."

"Mind your own business, *nanos*," Lydia said.

"Lydia is prickly, but she's not mean. And she'd never eat all this cheese," I said. "And you're not my grand-mother either. She was a lot of things but she wasn't cruel to people who didn't have it coming. So who are you?"

"I am Lydia, of course. Who else would I be?"

"Maria Griva," I said.

Jimmy did a double take. "Are you crazy?"

For the record, he was talking to me, the person who was exactly who they were supposed to be.

"Things are about to get crazier," I told him. "You should probably leave."

"And miss all this? I don't think so. What if I need it for a role someday?"

The odds of him playing someone who sees ghosts or a dead person shoehorned into a live person were … who knew. Possibly pretty high in porn. It wasn't like the story mattered. Probably everyone fast-forwarded through the slivers of plot to the happy ending.

"I am not this Maria whoever," Lydia said. "The *nanos* is right, you are crazy."

I ate cheese. Right under her nose.

She drooled a little.

"The ritual worked," I said, "only it didn't work on my grandmother. You were the one who ended up in a different body, because you were the one in Yiayia's coffin."

She swiped at my cheese. I moved it out of reach.

"No cheese for you," I said. "Not until you tell the truth."

"You know nothing."

So she wanted to play that game, did she? "I know you were having an affair with my grandmother—"

Jimmy choked.

"—and that you killed your husband after sex in the cemetery because he was concerned Yiayia changed her mind post-death about being slotted into another body, especially one that was almost as old as she was, new hips or not. You didn't care about the devil. That was an excuse to get him away from the board."

"During sex," she said. "He did not finish."

I knew it. "Out!"

"Virgin Mary," Jimmy said. "Average height people are a mess."

Maria/Lydia ignored him. "No! This is my body now. I like it. It is very young and attractive and healthy. You cannot make me leave."

"Lady, if someone put you in that body, somebody can force you out."

"I would like to see you try."

She had a point. My personal knowledge base didn't extend into woo-woo territory beyond the basics. Ousting a squatter wasn't in my wheelhouse. But maybe it was in Betty's. She knew things and people—even more things and people than I knew.

I dug my phone out of my bag.

"Same thing that will kill a slug will force a spirit out of a human hidey-hole," Betty said when I asked. "Salt."

Maria Griva glared at me from under her Lydia mask. The body hog didn't speak a lick of English.

"How do I apply it? Please don't say rectally."

Betty laughed. "Goodness me, no. Aren't you a funny one? All you have to do is give it a good sprinkle over the host."

"That's it?"

"You have to remember it's someplace it doesn't belong. That makes it easy to squeeze out, like a giant, overripe pimple. A bit of salt and the soul should pop right out. Works on most basic spells."

I thanked her for her help and shoved my phone back in its pocket. While I was wrist deep in darkness and leather, I felt around for the saltshaker I kept in there, a gift from the Man in Black.

A thought popped into my head. There was a thing I had to do, a suspicion that needed confirmation, before things maybe got ugly. I pulled out my hand and went over to the drawers where a thoughtful nurse had stashed Not-Lydia's belongings after they'd wrestled her into a hospital gown.

"What are you doing?"

"You stole something from me. I'm taking it back."

"Are you calling me a thief?"

The pink jar was in her cardigan pocket. She'd swiped it off my coffee table and crammed it into the pocket while she was scoffing my cheese. Cheese-eating thief.

"You took it," I asked her. "Why?"

"Because it is pretty."

I gave it a wiggle, placed it carefully in my bag. "Mine."

Maria/Lydia lunged across the bed. I jumped back.

"You have no idea what is in that jar," she hissed. "It is precious."

And just like that I knew what was in the jar. But this wasn't the time. We had unfinished business, Maria Griva, Lydia, and I. Or was it me? I wasn't sure and I didn't feel like Googling for a grammar lesson. My fingers touched the cold glass in my bag. The small shaker had come through for me before. Would it really solve Lydia's unwanted visitor problem?

"What is that?" Maria/Lydia eyed the saltshaker suspiciously.

"And you call yourself Greek," I said. "It's salt."

"What is it for?"

"This." My arm moved in an arc. The shaker flew out of my hand and hit Not-Lydia in the head.

"Ow," she said.

"That wasn't supposed to happen. Can I have my shaker back?"

"Give me the pink jar."

"No."

"I will keep this shaker. It is very nice. Silver and crystal, I think."

"Really?"

"Oh yes. It is good quality. Expensive."

So the Man in Black had access to high quality kitchenware that he could afford to give away to random women. Interesting. Not relevant to the situation, but definitely intriguing.

I reached for the shaker. She sat on it like a chicken on its eggs.

Any other time I might shove her over and grab the shaker, but I was tired. My lungs were still wonky from the smoke. My throat hurt. I'd been chased by an irate Englishman. My grandmother was dumped in the sea while wearing a yellow thong bikini, along with her sex toys. A woman sitting on my saltshaker was too much.

"I'll be back," I said.

I didn't go anywhere. Her IV bag caught my attention. Saline. Salt water. The concentration wasn't high but maybe it didn't need to be. Salt was salt. The great cosmic cleanser. I unhooked the bag, tipped it upside down, and wrenched off the doodad that connected to the tubing.

"You cannot do that!" Maria Griva said, using Lydia's mouth.

"Want to bet?"

I squished the bag. Water shot out, slapped her in the kisser. She yowled like a coyote and went diving under the bed. If Lydia made it out the other side, she'd be one big bruise.

"Get out," I said. The underside of the bed looked complicated and dangerous. A lot of hydraulic bits and pieces that made the bed move. Anyone bigger than Lydia would never fit.

"No!"

I crouched down and let her have it. Salty water splashed across her face. Her hand shot out. She'd made a fist. It nailed me in the eye. I fell back, plastic bag limp in my hand. I was out of energy and out of saline. It hadn't worked. Maria Griva was still stuck inside Lydia's skin. The saline had only pissed her off.

Maria/Lydia crawled out. While my eye was puffing up like a Kardashian's butt implants, she sat on me. Her hands found my neck.

"You are the worst," she said. "You are not worthy of your grandmother's blood. You have the devil in you, like my husband."

"Yiayia loved me. Can you say the same?"

Her fingers tightened around my throat. My lungs burned. Tears streamed down my cheeks. Strangulation really stank.

Stupid hospital. Every time I wound up here it was drama and a pain in my rear. At least if she managed to kill me, which was looking more likely by the second, I was already in a hospital. Silver lining, or something like that.

"Help," I whispered.

"No one will help you," Maria Griva told me.

"I will," Jimmy Kontos said.

Maria/Lydia swing around. Jimmy flung the saltshaker at her. Grains of salt pelted her face.

She screamed.

Footsteps sounded in the hall. Nurses ran in. They hauled Maria/Lydia off me and tried to wrestle her back into bed. She flopped around like a toddler who'd just been told chicken nuggets weren't on the breakfast menu. Jimmy continued shaking salt on her. Like all Greeks he went heavy on the sodium. The nurses didn't stop him. They'd been raised on folk medicine and didn't see basic culinary ingredients as a safety issue.

"I don't know what I'm doing," he said.

"Keep doing it," I urged him. A nurse was fawning over me. I brushed her away and got up. My throat was going to be sore for days. I'd be on a liquid diet for the next week. Good thing I liked soup.

"But what am I doing?" he asked.

"You wouldn't believe me if I told you."

"Probably not."

Maria Griva kicked Lydia's legs in the air. "The Virgin Mary sucks *poutsas* in hell," she shouted.

"I can't tell if that's a regular Greek insult or she's watched *The Exorcist* one too many times," I said.

"The price of cheese is just too damn high," she yelled.

"Pretty sure that's a meme," I said.

Then Lydia passed out.

Not Maria Griva, though. She was herself again: round, wretched, and this time she didn't have a slipper to throw. She tried bowling herself back into Lydia's body. Not happening.

"Virgin Mary," she said. "I had plans for that body. Big, naked plans. I was going to eat all the cheese."

"You couldn't eat cheese before?" I asked her.

"Cheese made it so I could not *kaka*. And the price … *po-po* … What happened to the price of cheese? But in a young, new body I could eat all the cheese I wanted."

This time the swirly hole opened up in the hospital floor. Blacker than a starless night. Large enough to swallow the bed, if that's what it was here for. Which it wasn't.

Nobody noticed except me and Maria Griva.

I jumped backward.

"What is that?" Maria Griva wanted to know.

"Ah," I said. "It's—"

Konstantinos Grivas appeared. "Maria! My love!"

His wife rolled her eyes. "You. What are you doing here?"

"By the way," I said, trying to be helpful. "Your wife killed you. Sorry about that."

"I know," he said. "I heard her confession when she was squatting in the girl. I recognized her foul disposition, even in another body. But I do not care. I still love you, Maria."

"The Virgin Mary's *kolos*," Maria Griva said, clearly unhappy.

The Hole of Judgment got a lip-lock on her and sucked her right up. Didn't even give her time to flail and curse.

Konstantinos Grivas leaped in after her.

"Thank you," he called out to me. "I will make sure others know you helped me."

"Wait, what?" I yelped. "No!"

The floor went back to being a floor, spilled salt and all.

In the bed, Lydia slept. Her pulse was stable. Her oxygen level was normal. She'd be fine.

"I have to go," I told Jimmy.

"You going to explain any of this?"

"Any of what?" I did my best dumb act. "Must be aftereffects from those edibles you ate the other night."

He whistled low. "You could be right." He thought about it a moment. "I've got to get myself more of those."

———

Despite the nurses' fussing, I left. I had somewhere to be and someone to talk to.

I found Kyria Eugenia in her yard, sweeping as though her life depended on it. A lot of enthusiasm for a woman who was mostly burns.

"You've lost Yiayia haven't you?" I said. "You're just going around, asking random people if they're her."

"We had a code phrase."

"Gangbang? I hate to tell you this, but tons of people know about those. You won't find her."

"The ritual worked, I know it."

"Oh, it definitely worked."

I told her about Kyria Maria and Lydia's body. And the part where I'd sorted out the problem with a little help from someone who wasn't exactly a friend.

She brightened up. "It worked?"

"I thought you just said it did! You sounded positive."

"It is best to always be confident, even when you are wrong. I hoped it worked but I was not positive. But now you are telling me it did. So where is Foutoula?"

"Trapped somewhere. I'm sure she would have shown up in Vicky Niki's body, just like you intended, if she could have."

"Can you find her? I will pay. They say you can find anything."

"I couldn't take your money," I told her.

I knew exactly where Yiayia was. And the more I thought about it, the more I realized I knew where Angela was, too.

CHAPTER TWENTY-ONE

"You figured it out," Betty said. "Where your missing friend is, I mean. You're broadcasting like crazy. Go on back then. The car will be waiting."

This time she gave me doughnut holes for the trip. Every hole turned out to be a different flavor, and every hole was hot until the bag was empty.

Magic was real, and it was in my baked goods.

I still had the key Sir Teddy Duckworth's neighbor had given me. I parked three blocks away and knocked on Charlie Brown's door.

"Look at you then, you're back. And you've got the key, too. I thought you were buggered the other night when Duckworth was chasing you. Couldn't believe my eyes when that fancy car drove itself right up to the door. Did you find out anything about Mavis yet?"

"Not yet, but I know where she is."

"Let me get a pen and paper," he said. "The marbles aren't always where they're supposed to be, these days."

"No need. She's close by."

"How close, then?"

"About from here to there." I gestured at the Duckworth house.

He didn't look so sure. "If Mavis was there I'd know."

"She's there. I wouldn't bet your life or mine on it, but I'd bet Sir Teddy's."

"Good enough for me. We should get going now, before that tosspot gets home."

"We?"

"This sounds like a rescue mission. I always wanted to be part of a rescue mission. Plus it seems to me like you could use some backup."

Who was I to deny him his harmless wish?

I let us in through the front door and gave Charlie back his key. He dropped it in his shirt pocket.

"All right then, where is Mavis?"

"In there, most likely." I nodded toward the living room with its big TV and wall-to-wall castles.

We moved into the living room. It smelled like fish and chips.

"You think he stuffed her in one of the walls or under the floorboards?"

"Close but no." I got my phone out, swiped over to a magnifying glass app, tapped. I handed him the phone. "Pick a castle, then pick a window."

Charlie followed my instructions. He bent down and peered through the window of a castle I didn't recognize. It sure was pretty though.

"I don't see anything except the inside of a castle. That's some good details. He's a minging cockwomble but he sure can make things."

"Pick another window."

What if I was wrong?

He followed my instruction. "Oi, take a look at this." He handed back my phone.

I crouched down, peered into the castle through my phone. Inside the front bedroom was a miniature woman, staring back at me. The woman raised her middle finger and lunged at the window, at odds with her lavender twinset and pearls. Her hair was trapped in a French twist. Her sensible heels said she wasn't comfortable going barefoot in a castle, or that she hoped to be rescued soon.

The thrill of uncovering the truth rippled through me. Followed by fear. How was I supposed to save a tiny woman?

One by one, I worked my way through the castles and discovered more women. Sir Teddy Duckworth had a type. Women with means, by the looks of it, and tasteful, sedate wardrobes. No wonder he was attracted to Angela. Angela, who I found tearing down a wall in a replica of some famous Austrian castle. Her face lit up when she realized I wasn't Sir Teddy. She yelled something but she was too tiny. I held up a finger and told her wait.

I addressed the room.

"All of you listen up. My name is Allie Callas and I'm here to save you. I don't know how yet, exactly, but I'll find a way."

"That's what you think," Sir Teddy Duckworth said from the open doorway.

I dropped my phone. "Crap."

"If that's an order, I can do it," Charlie Brown said. "I'd be glad to, under the circumstances."

"Knew you'd be back, didn't I?" Duckworth said. He looked pleased with himself. Like all his paranoid fantasies had borne fruit. Which they had, damn it. "All I had to do was park one street over and call in sick for a couple of days."

"Aren't you a special and smart big boy?" I said. Clearly the man had issues with women, so I decided not to rein in my inner sarcastic smartass. Terror washed over me anyway. Duckworth was a big man, and I wasn't confident my pepper spray had enough juice left to take him down. Coming here without a weapon was an idiot move, which made me queen of the idiots. If Sir Teddy wanted to shoot me with his ray gun and stuff me in castle, he could. "I bet your mother would be proud. Where is she, by the way?"

He indicated toward the topmost castle on his shelves. Smaller than the others, it was blocky and less polished. Everyone had to start somewhere, I guess.

"Hever Castle," Sir Teddy said. "Perfect for that old witch."

"Mavis better not be dead," Charlie said.

"Relax, you old fart. She's still alive. She's less of a pain in the arse now, I can tell you. Always bitching about my arts and crafts, calling me some kind of fairy because I liked making things more than I liked sports. I'm no fairy. I'm just crafty, that's all."

"Sorry your mother is a homophobe who hates crafts," I said, "but that's no reason to shrink her down to the size of a bee and stuff her in a castle. Her or the other women. How did you do it, and why?"

I was buying time. For what, I didn't know. Nobody was riding to the rescue. Leo didn't know I'd left Merope. I was on my own, unless Charlie counted. Maybe he could fling poop like a monkey and incapacitate Duckworth.

"Castles are made to be lived in, aren't they?" Sir Teddy said. "Mine are so bleedin' good I didn't fancy putting dolls in them. Dolls make the castles look cheap. Like they're some sort of toys. My castles aren't toys. They're perfect replicas."

"How did you shrink the women?"

He shrugged. "It's magic, innit?"

"Magic? Really? Aren't you a construction worker?"

"That's hurtful, that's what that is. Construction workers can do other things as well. We don't all sit around watching the footy, drinking pints. All my mates have other hobbies. Building castles and magic are mine."

"So you want me to believe you're some kind of magician, like Harry Potter?"

"Harry Potter was a wizard, not a magician. I'm not a magician either. Magicians perform tricks. What I do is real."

He had a point. Full-size women were now the height of a pea. That had happened somehow, and I was sure it wasn't because he'd tossed them in a hot dryer. So that left magic.

"Well, if you could turn them all back to regular women, that would be great. Otherwise you'll end up in prison where they frown on things like magic and building castles."

He frowned. "Why would I do that? No one's ever gonna find out. All I have to do is shrink you two and that's it. Problem solved."

"People know I'm here."

"What people?"

"Woo-woo people."

As I said it I realized it was true. Betty and Jack were totally woo-woo. The question was: were they woo-woo enough to track me down and zap me back to regular size, along with all the other women?

"Woo-woo people," he scoffed. "Ten quid says there's no such people that know you're here."

"How did you wind up performing magic?" *Buy time, Allie. Buy time. Find a solution.*

"I told you, that witch who brought me into this world."

"Mavis weren't no witch," Charlie said. "She could be bitchy, I'll give you that, but I never saw her doing no magic."

Duckworth rolled his eyes. "This fookin' knob." He clicked his fingers and his neighbor vanished. Duckworth bent down, plucked something off the floor.

Charlie.

"I've been sick and tired of that bugger's yapping mouth since I moved in here. Should have done this years ago, when I did my Mum. They could have talked each other's ears off in their own private prison."

This was bad. I was down my only ally. Now it was all up to me. Screw it up and I'd wind up in a castle, along with his other miniatures.

From where I was standing, escaping from Duckworth's art projects looked easy enough. They were small enough that I could climb out a window and flee. Then my brain mentally shrunk me down and I recalculated. I'd never be able to escape. The reason the other women hadn't made a run for it was because they'd die if they jumped. Size matters.

"Which castle is he going in?" I asked.

Sir Teddy held up his neighbor between two fingers. "He's not." He popped the man into his mouth and swallowed. "Needs more salt."

I gawked at him, horrified and a little bit disgusted. He'd eaten a man. Murdered him. Probably murdered. How long could a person survive in stomach acid anyway?

My options were limited to nada, nothing, and sweet FA.

What did I have?

Keys. Phone. Possibly half-empty pepper spray. Lip balm. Old receipts. A notebook and pen. Saltshaker. And low level working knowledge of woo-woo things.

At this juncture I had nothing to lose. Go big or never go home. So I scrounged up every spare speck of energy and channeled it into my leg, and swung from the hip, nailing Sir Teddy Duckworth square in the goobers. I'd kicked him so hard he'd smell crotch sweat for the rest of his life.

He fell to his knees, cradling his cracked nuts. Tears raced down his cheekbones. His bottom jaw dangled. He cried like a baby with a full diaper and an empty belly.

It was an opening. And here I was with a saltshaker.

"More salt, you said?"

I wrenched off the lid and tossed a handful at his face, hoping some would make it into his mouth and down his throat.

He coughed. He swallowed salt and tears.

If this didn't work, Charlie was going to be in deep *kaka* —literally.

Should I run? Probably that would be smart. That way if my plan failed I'd be at a safe distance by the time Sir Teddy's nausea and blinding pain subsided. I could return later with backup. Not the police. There was no good way to explain that a wizard had shrunk a handful of women using magic and now they were imprisoned in his minia- ture castles.

Maybe Leo would come with me. If he could handle me seeing ghosts, then it was only a small leap to accepting woman-shrinking wizards.

And then Sir Teddy Duckworth exploded.

CHAPTER TWENTY-TWO

BLOOD SPLATTERED. Buckets of the stuff. It made a woofing sound as it hit the walls and floor. At the same time, Sir Teddy Duckworth's ribcage burst open with an ominous *crack*. His lungs slapped a lamp and then slid to the carpet in the least sexiest pole dance in history. No longer powered by his brain, which was suddenly lounging on the recliner, his pelvis and legs slumped sideways.

Standing the wreckage was Charlie Brown, back to his regular size. He wolf-whistled.

"Blimey! The whole world was sixes and sevens there for a minute. Am I dead? I had a handful of his dangly bit for a moment, but then he swallowed.

"You're still alive," I said, relieved. "But I think Sir Teddy needs a doctor."

He checked out the state of the room. "Bit of an improvement, if you ask me."

We were covered in blood, guts, and bits of food. Charlie had ham in his hair.

I wasn't freaking out. Could be it was shock. Sir Teddy Duckworth was dead but I'd saved Charlie. And now that I knew salt worked to break certain magic spells, I had a way to save the women he'd shrunk.

"Everybody out of your castles," I said. "I'm going to pass around a plate, and when I raise it to the castle door, hop aboard."

I'd like to think I heard cheering, but I couldn't be sure.

———

The saltshaker was down to a few sad grains. Definitely in dire need of a refill before I could return the women to their regular sizes. The carpet squelched as I picked my way across the living room, avoiding lumps of Duckworth. In the kitchen, I found salt and refilled my shaker. Then I got to work sprinkling the tiny women with grains of sodium snow. But first I carried the plate to a room that wasn't decorated with bits o' Sir Teddy.

One at a time, they popped back to normal. They were thin but healthy. Duckworth had fed them crumbs and drops of water served in Barbie's plastic cups.

All in all, there were twenty women on the plate when I was done, including Angela and Duckworth's mother, Mavis. Angela wasn't a demonstrative woman, but she looked at me like she'd hug me if she were a completely different person. "I knew you would come."

"Thank Alfred," I said. "He insisted I find you."

"I tried to call you," she said. "Right after that *kolotripas* zapped me, before he dropped me in his ridiculous toy castle."

The phone had rung. When no one was on the other end, that's when I first got the inkling that things weren't okay. I apologized for not riding to the rescue sooner.

"I think I am going to quit men," Angela said. "Unless you find me a good one." She gave me an expectant look.

No. No-o-o-o.

"Angela …"

"I will pay you as much as you want."

"I think I know a guy," I said.

"Introduce me." She looked me up and down, suddenly noticing I was covered in a layer of Duckworth. "After you have a bath."

———

One at a time, the missing women used my phone to call their loved ones. I told them where Duckworth had stashed their phones and handbags. Angela called for a limo to take her to the airport. Charlie was sitting with Mavis, who didn't strike me as entirely unhappy that she'd need a carpet cleaner to suck up what was left of her son.

"I'm sorry your son exploded," I said to her.

"And he was such a nice boy," she said. "Everything went wrong after he discovered glitter."

"Kids love glitter. There's no stopping them."

"He was thirty years old at the time," she said.

Charlie stood. Things creaked. He made a face but he didn't complain about his feet. Definitely not a Greek bone in his body. "First thing's first, I'm going to make a cuppa. Then we're going to clean this place."

My phone rang.

"Dinner tonight?" Leo asked.

"As long as it's not meat."

———

My clothes were clean, thanks to Mavis Duckworth's superior laundry skills. We'd scrubbed every speck of Sir Teddy out of the living room, and then Mavis called the garbage service to haul away her son's arts and crafts collection. Not a sentimental woman, Mavis Duckworth.

"I bet I could find a buyer," I said.

"No need for any of that," she said. "I prefer the satisfaction of knowing his life's work is rotting in a landfill."

"Are you really a witch?"

"What do you think, dear?"

"Your laundry skills say yes."

"Then you should trust your instincts. Now, what can I do to say thank you for freeing me from that wretched prison? A little token? Something of Sir Teddy's?"

I thought about it. Sir Teddy Duckworth had nothing I wanted. But he had something from Popi's wish list.

"How about a book?"

———

Eventually, I fell down on my own couch. I closed my eyes.

"Are you dead?" Yiorgos Dakis asked.

"Yes."

"You are lying."

"Go away," I said. "Please."

Dakis planted himself in front of the couch. He was up to his saggy knees in coffee table.

"I don't know why you're here," I said.

"It is my business, yes? It is unfinished."

"But what is it?"

"Who can say? Not me. All I did was die, by accident, on Foutoula's grave!"

A light came on in my head.

"You were part of it, weren't you?"

"Part of what?"

"This whole scheme to bring Yiayia back."

"Of course. She was one of my friends and also my

lover, when it suited her. That's why I always went to her grave to—"

"Stop talking right now," I said.

My body complained as I rolled off the couch. It wanted to stay where the cushions were soft and warm. As I stood, Dead Cat appeared, claiming my spot. Cats: dead or alive, they're all the same.

I found my handbag where I'd left it, lying on the living room floor. The pink jar was inside. I set it on the coffee table.

Dead Cat began to rumble.

"Do you really want to bring Yiayia back?" I asked.

"Of course!"

My grandmother hadn't come back because she couldn't. Reading between the lines, her ghost had pestered the hell out of Roger Wilson, until he was driven to suck her up into one of his salt prisons after his attempts to acquire her body and silence her that way had failed.

That she'd come back so soon to annoy Wilson told me either she'd been murdered or she had some other unfinished business of vital, to her, importance.

Maybe there was some other explanation. Wilson got sucked into the swirly hole, so it wasn't like I could ask him.

But I could ask Yiayia.

My hand shook as I wiggled the cork.

"What are you doing?" Yiorgos Dakis asked. He was still up to his knees in table.

"Move back."

"Why?"

For a moment I struggled with the cork lid, then it popped free. Mist shot up and out of the jar. It bounced off the walls, a rogue ping-pong ball.

Purring like a train, Dead Cat stood, stretched.

The mist quit bouncing. It stopped in the middle of the

room, then slowly solidified in one familiar shape. Dead Cat leaped into the figure's arms.

Yiorgos Dakis' mouth opened and closed. "Foutoula!" He started to fade. "*Gamo tin putana* …"

He disappeared, leaving me with the jar's former occupant.

"Hello, Yiayia," I said.

THANK YOU FOR READING GOLDEN GHOULS!

If you'd like to be notified about special prices on new releases, subscribe to my newsletter at http://eepurl.com/ZSeuL or Like my page on Facebook: https://www.facebook.com/alexkingbooks

If you enjoyed the book, or if you didn't enjoy the book, please consider leaving a review. You could help another reader fall in love … or save them from making a terrible mistake.

All my best,
Alex A. King

ALSO BY ALEX A. KING

Disorganized Crime (Kat Makris #1)

Trueish Crime (Kat Makris #2)

Doing Crime (Kat Makris #3)

In Crime (Kat Makris #4)

Outta Crime (Kat Makris #5)

Night Crime (Kat Makris #6)

Good Crime (Kat Makris #7)

White Crime (Kat Makris #8)

Christmas Crime (Kat Makris #9)

Seven Days of Friday (Women of Greece #1)

One and Only Sunday (Women of Greece #2)

Freedom the Impossible (Women of Greece #3)

Light is the Shadow (Women of Greece #4)

No Peace in Crazy (Women of Greece #5)

Summer of the Red Hotel (Women of Greece #6)

Rotten Little Apple (Women of Greece #7)

The Last of June (Women of Greece #8)

Family Ghouls (Greek Ghouls #1)

Royal Ghouls (Greek Ghouls #2)

Stolen Ghouls (Greek Ghouls #3)

Pride and All This Prejudice

Printed in Great Britain
by Amazon